Spiritual Drafting

Susie

Dreams Do

Come true.

William [illegible]

Spiritual Drafting

When One Person Has the Power to Change Everything

WM. TODD NICHOLS

SPIRITUAL DRAFTING
WHEN ONE PERSON HAS THE POWER
TO CHANGE EVERYTHING

Copyright © 2019 Wm. Todd Nichols.

All rights reserved. No part of this book may be used or reproduced by any means, graphic, electronic, or mechanical, including photocopying, recording, taping or by any information storage retrieval system without the written permission of the author except in the case of brief quotations embodied in critical articles and reviews.

iUniverse books may be ordered through booksellers or by contacting:

iUniverse
1663 Liberty Drive
Bloomington, IN 47403
www.iuniverse.com
1-800-Authors (1-800-288-4677)

Because of the dynamic nature of the Internet, any web addresses or links contained in this book may have changed since publication and may no longer be valid. The views expressed in this work are solely those of the author and do not necessarily reflect the views of the publisher, and the publisher hereby disclaims any responsibility for them.

This is a work of fiction. All of the characters, names, incidents, organizations, and dialogue in this novel are either the products of the author's imagination or are used fictitiously.

Any people depicted in stock imagery provided by Getty Images are models, and such images are being used for illustrative purposes only. Certain stock imagery © Getty Images.

ISBN: 978-1-5320-6965-9 (sc)
ISBN: 978-1-5320-6966-6 (e)

Library of Congress Control Number: 2019902266

Print information available on the last page.

iUniverse rev. date: 02/28/2019

Contents

Prologue

Mike McConnell asked his best friend and pit crew chief Doug Schlipp, "Do you think about reincarnation?"

"I have before. I'll hear a story of some supernatural event that took place. It gets you wondering if there's more to death than we know," replied Doug.

"Man, I think about it all the time!"

***

North Wilkesboro Speedway, North Carolina

April 9, 1995, the Winston Cup Series

The event was the First Union 400. Mike McConnell, four-time Winston Cup champion, had raced two hundred miles, and he was running in the twentieth position.

McConnell complained to his pit crew chief through his microphone headset that his car was very loose. "Doug, man! Car's running too loose! I'm having trouble keeping the car on the track. I need a sway bar adjustment and a fresh set of tires."

Mike made an unexpected pit stop. The pit crew sweat as they worked to change the tires. While it was only

April, the North Carolina humidity that would become oppressive in the dreaded dog days of August had made an early appearance. Mike wiped sweat off his face with the back of his right hand. The high-pitched squeal of the glorified electric drills used to remove the lug nuts mingled with the low hum of the crowd in the background. Moving swiftly, the pit crew changed all four tires and set the sway bar adjustment. They lowered the jack lever so that all four tires were on the ground and swiftly moved away from the car. McConnell's right hand was on the stick shift, and his fingers were wrapped around the ball-shaped handle. He slammed the car into gear and spun the tires. A haze of smoke appeared from them.

The pit crew chief said to McConnell as he drove down pit row, "Twelve seconds flat! How's that for a pit stop!"

McConnell replied, "Now it's up to me, boys. Great job!"

***

Two hundred and five miles into the race, McConnell's new right front tire blew, causing him to head straight for the wall. He gripped the steering wheel with terror, preparing for the impact.

The fans heard a loud crash. As they looked with wonder, they were concerned whether McConnell was okay.

The front of the car smashed in, and everything went black.

About the Book

WM.TODD NICHOLS was born in Michigan and raised in a small town called Eau Claire. He was inspired by his Mother & Father believing in a spiritual connection with thy self and the Universe. He loves his family and enjoys spending time with his wife and children.

Acknowledgement

I am very grateful to those who reacted to the early drafts of this manuscript and their support throughout the process. Especially my wife Jennifer, son Tony, and daughter Brianna, my neighbors, Bret and Laura Hendrie. Also, thanks to Nancy Lahage who read the manuscript while fixing some of the errors you were the first person that got me going in the right direction. Special thank you to Jo Herman for all that she does for the American Veterans, for helping me stay on track to finish my book, and for all the support you've given me in my life. I also want to thank my deceased parents Jim and Gwen Nichols. I wouldn't have been able to accomplish the book without all of their life guidance and love which gave me the strength to write this book. I'm very grateful to my sister Joelene VonKoenig for all the support and spiritual connection that you continually give to me. I'm very grateful to my Brother-in-law Doug VonKoenig, for being a big support through the process of publishing the book. Finally I would like to thank Betty Ivers for being the first of the four editors that took on the task of editing my book professionally. Because of you helping me that gave me the confidence to move forward and find a publishing company.

The whole project took seven years, between working fulltime and raising a family. I was faced with many challenges. It's very rewarding to see it all come together and I'm grateful that I did not quit.

1

Convincing the Parents

Jake moved the toy tractor across the carpet, growling as he made fake engine sounds. He heard the anchorman say that Mike had been dead seven years, as long as Jake had been alive. He stopped playing with the tractor. He watched the film footage that showed Mike getting into his car on that last fateful race day. Jake stared at the NASCAR great, a racer who seemed larger than life. He felt vaguely unsettled as he wondered why he found the dead racer so important to him.

"Jake!" his mom called. "Come on down right now! Your breakfast is getting cold!"

Jake raced into the kitchen to sit down with his family. Jake, the oldest of the two siblings, ate his waffles with gusto. He looked over at Vinci, his six-year-old sister. He could tell she liked her breakfast as well. For the longest time, Jake had been interested in a NASCAR great named Mike McConnell. He'd just seen yet another report on him on ESPN. He even dreamed about the racer, who'd crashed and burned way back in 1995. He swallowed some more of his waffle, looked out the kitchen window, saw a bird fly by, and turned to his mom, Julia.

He asked, "Hey, Mom, you ever heard of Mike McConnell?"

His father, Dan, stopped chewing his waffle; he looked at Julia, shrugging his shoulders, and said, "I think he was a famous NASCAR driver."

"That's right," Julia said. "Why are you asking, honey?"

"They were talking about him on the TV before I came into the kitchen," Jake said.

"Now, I could tell you about some golf legends like Ben Hogan," Dan said.

Dan was a golf pro at a local golf course called Brook Wood. He gave golf lessons and was responsible for the operation of the business.

"No, thanks, Dad," Jake interrupted.

"What! My son doesn't like golf? Come on. You're killing me!"

Jake laughed. "You tell us about those guys all the time, Dad."

"And you can't get enough of them, can you, son?"

Jake laughed.

Jake wolfed down the last of his waffle. His parents said their goodbyes, and then he and his sister rushed to the car. Julia also ran to the car. She loaded the kids in and drove off pretty fast because they were running late for school.

Julia was a third-grade teacher at Jake and Vinci's school, Johnson Elementary.

For the next several hours at school, Jake found it hard to concentrate. He kept thinking about that racer, Mike

McConnell. When lunch finally came, he ate quickly and went out to the playground to look for his friends.***

Jake grabbed five of his closest friends—Jimmy, John, Frank, Bobby, and Mike. Jake explained to them that they were about to have a footrace around the school. He assigned them racing numbers, acting as if they were race car drivers. Mike was standing in front of them with his hand in the air. "On your marks, get set, and go!"

The race started, with Jimmy and Bobby getting a big jump on everybody. When they came up to the first turn, Jimmy was in first, Bobby in second, and Jake in third, while Frank and John followed.

Jake was right on Bobby's heels going into the second turn. He passed Bobby, going around the swing set.

They came down the straightaway, and Jake and Jimmy were shoulder to shoulder. They were bumping and rubbing each other as Mike took his white T-shirt off and started waving it like the checkered flag.

Jake crossed the finish line first, pumping both of his fists in the air. He shouted, "I won! I won!"

Jimmy ran up to Jake and said, "You cheated. You pushed me!"

"No, I didn't push you. I rubbed you, and rubbing is racing," said Jake.

***

The first-grade teacher, Joann, and Jake's mother watched the whole race. They were both stunned to see how Jake took control and gave each person racing numbers and by his comment about rubbing in racing.

Jake's mother said, "We don't watch racing. I wonder where all that came from. Now, if he acted out the master's tournament at Augusta, *that* I would understand. But to pretend he is a race car driver is kind of strange."

The bell rang, and recess was over. The kids lined up at the door to get to ready to go back to class.

"I will let you know if I see anything else like that again from Jake," Joann said.

"I'd really appreciate it," replied Julia.

***

That evening, Jake's family sat down to eat dinner together.

All of a sudden, Jake blurted out a question. "Hey, Mom and Dad, can I have a go-kart? The kind that races, not the kind you drive in the driveway? It needs to be high performance and race ready."

Dan held a forkful of spaghetti by his mouth. He shook his head. "Where does this sudden interest in racing come from? Who have you been talking to, Jake?"

"Dad, it's something I think I would be good at, and I have not been talking to anybody. It just popped into my head."

"You should have seen him on the playground today; Jake and his friends had a little footrace. They acted as if they were race car drivers. Jake even gave each one of them racing numbers," Julia said.

"Jake, I know nothing about racing, and you're not old enough yet to have a speedy go-kart," Dan said.

"Yeah, dear, we want you to be happy. Let your father and me talk about this and see when the time is right to do this," Julia said.

Jake protested and threw a fit because he didn't like the answer his parents gave him.

He went out to the garage to get his Big Wheel and toys out. He placed the toys in a perimeter around the driveway in the form of a racetrack. Jake had a pogo stick on one corner and a soccer ball in the next corner. He had a hockey stick and a football in the other corners. Jake sat in his Big Wheel and started pedaling his little three-wheeler very fast around the racetrack.

He came up to his first turn and slid his back wheels around the pogo stick, throwing little bits of stone into the grass while he continued to pedal very fast. He came up to turn 2, leaned hard into the corner, and flew around the soccer ball, still pedaling fast, as he headed down the back straightaway. He had his head low to the steering wheel to keep the wind drag down. To go faster, he came up to turn 3 and slid the back end around again without touching the hockey stick as he kept the momentum up with a good pace. Coming up to turn 4, he gripped the steering wheel tightly and leaned into the last turn, just cutting the edge of the football and never touching it. He got on the pedals and powered that little three-wheeler past the very first lap. Jake continued to ride hard for thirty-five minutes, until he was exhausted.

***

Julia sighed as she stood at the window. Jake was racing in the driveway again. She was unsettled, even scared. He'd been at this for three weeks. He'd even changed the paint job on his Big Wheel.

"Hey honey," Dan Said coming up behind her. She took his right hand in hers and gave it a gentle squeeze. "Have you noticed how much time Jake, has been spending in the drive way?" Julia asked.

"Yes, I have noticed. Sometimes I have to pick up a hockey stick so I can back out of the driveway to go to work," Dan said.

"Well, I think we need to talk about this go-kart again; he is showing us how much he loves racing," Julia said.

"Yes, and every night, we get a good education at the dinner table on the past NASCAR greats! Where does he get that information from?" Dan asked.

Julia shrugged her shoulders. "I don't know."

"You know, I looked up on the computer what he told us about Fireball Roberts, and he was correct about everything he said about him."

"Dan, are you sure? That is really strange."

"Yes, I read it all. It gave me a big chill when I was reading it."

"That is weird."

"There is a go-kart racing store in Three Oaks. Do you want to go there and take a look around?" he asked.

"Yes, I think so. Why don't you go first and talk to them and see if we can afford this. Find out everything we need to know about the sport," she said.

"Okay, good idea. I will stop by there after work tomorrow."

***

The sun momentarily blinded Dan when it reflected off the MRP racing store in Three Oaks. He blinked rapidly, opened the door, and walked in, ready to learn all there was to know about go-kart racing for kids.

Tony came over to Dan, extended his hand, and introduced himself as the owner. He asked, "What can I do for you?"

Dan looked around briefly before answering Tony. He saw a photo of a racetrack on the wall that looked like it was taken from an aerial view. The room was stocked with racing equipment, helmets, and uniforms, and on the floor were racing go-karts.

Tony was man of medium height; in his late sixties, he was a little out of shape and had silver hair. He had very little hair on his chin and a mustache, which he kept shaved close.

"Yes. My name is Dan, and I have a seven-year-old son who has a huge interest in racing. I wonder what you guys have to offer."

Tony showed Dan the type of go-karts they had. The Birel brand was very popular. Dan knelt down and examined the go-kart. The kart sat very low to the ground, with the engine behind it. The tires were small and made for the hard surface with no tire tread on them. The colors on the kart were typically red, white, and blue. On the front of the steering wheel, there was a place to put your racing number and another down on the side of the kart. The engines were different in size. On the nine horsepower, the speed would reach thirty-five miles per hour; with the twenty-nine-horsepower engine, the speed would average fifty miles per hour or better; and the Rotax kart's thirty-nine horsepower's speed averaged sixty-five to seventy miles per hour.

The karts had won championships across the world; there were pictures and trophies to support his information. The store had the full setup: racing helmets and uniforms. Dan got a tour of their shop. In addition, they had a complete support system for parts and professional help in the setup of the kart.

"We also have one-on-one private lessons," mentioned Tony.

Tony pointed out a picture on the wall that Dan had first seen when he walked in. He was pointing and showing Dan how to turn into a corner and how to get power coming out of the turn by accelerating at the right time.

"You and your son can use this racetrack anytime. I personally own it. There is a one-hundred-dollar annual fee to the track for upkeep, and also this is where we practice and sometimes race. We have another track in North Liberty, Indiana," Tony said.

"How often do you guys race?" Dan asked.

"Every Saturday and every other Sunday. We can even fit you into a kart so the two of you can race," Tony said.

"How much does a couple of karts cost?" asked Dan.

"The average price starts at two thousand dollars for one and can go up to four thousand, all depends on the size of the engine."

Dan smiled. "I think we need to stick to just one right now. You gave me a lot to think about and to talk over with my wife. I'll be in touch."

Dan walked out of the racing store. He had a good feeling that this was the place where Jake needed to get started. He jumped into his SUV, knowing that dinner was going to be cold when he got home. On the way home,

Dan was excited about this new adventure he was starting with his son.

When he got home, he parked in the street in front of their house because Jake was in the driveway, racing his Big Wheel.

"Hey, big guy, you sure are wearing down the wheels on that Big Wheel!"

"Hi, Dad. Where have you been? It's late."

"Oh, I've been shopping."

"What kind of shopping?"

"Car shopping."

"You're going to get a new car?"

"Yeah, something like that, champ. Do you know where Mom is?"

"I think she and Vinci are reading together in the kitchen. What kind of car are you looking at, Dad?"

"A red one." Dan smiled really big.

"Cool."

Dan went into the house to find Julia, who was reading to Vinci like Jake said she was.

Dan opened the refrigerator door to find his dinner. "Hey, ladies, what are you reading?" he asked.

"Hi, Dad. We're reading about the three little pigs and the big bad wolf," said Vinci.

"Oh, yeah. Has the wolf huffed and puffed yet?"

"Yep, and blew their house down," she said with a grin.

"What did you find out in Three Oaks?" Julia asked.

Dan told Julia everything about the kart store.

Julia laughed. "You seem to be very excited about this."

"I am excited about what they have to offer. A new guy who knows nothing about the sport has a chance because they will work with us. It's not like they're going to sell us the kart and send us on our way. They are going to help us get started, and that makes me feel better about the whole thing. And also it will give Jake and me some quality time together."

"You know your time will be spent at the track now instead of the golf course?"

Dan smiled. "I know. We are doing this for Jake and maybe a little for me."

"What do you mean, Dan, when you say 'a little for me'?"

"Well, all that time I missed with my dad. We know how much he loved racing. Maybe it will make me feel better getting out to the track and doing something for Jake because he has that same passion that my dad had. Why not let him enjoy it?"

"I agree. When do we want to talk to him about this?"

"Jake is going to get a kart!" Vinci said with a big smile.

"Yes, and keep quiet until we talk to him about it," Julia said. Then she winked.

Vinci put her finger to her lips. "I won't tell, Mom."

"Do you want to tell him now?" Dan asked.

"Yeah, let's tell him now!" Vinci said with excitement.

"Okay, let's," Julia said.

"Vinci, will you go tell your brother we want to talk to him?" he continued. "And remember—don't say anything," Dan said.

"Okay, Dad, I won't," Vinci said with a smirk on her face.

***

Vinci opened the door to look for Jake. He was not playing in the driveway anymore. She walked outside with a big smile on her face, and she started creeping around, looking for him. Hands up and her fingers bent, she was ready to scare Jake when she found him. Then Jake popped out from behind the bushes and grabbed Vinci by the waist.

"I got you!"

Vinci screamed. "How did you know I was coming outside?"

"I was watching from the window, and I saw you walking to the door."

"Well, Mom and Dad want you to come inside; they want to talk to you," Vinci said with her lip sticking way out.

"What do they want?"

Vinci got a big smile on her face and started swaggering back and forth as she walked to the door. "That's for me to know and you to find out!"

Jake started running to the front door. Vinci saw he'd gotten the lead on her.

"Hey, Jake, I was just kidding. Mom and Dad don't want to see you!"

"Ah, Vinci, I don't believe you."

"No, really." She pushed Jake back and started running to the door.

"You little cheater!"

Vinci reached out to grab the door handle, but Dan opened it. Vinci lost her balance and fell on her face. Jake started laughing hysterically. Vinci was embarrassed, listening to her brother laugh, and upset at herself because it didn't goes as planned.

"Are you okay, Vinci?" Jake asked.

Vinci started laughing. "Yeah, I'm okay."

"You two are goofballs," Dan commented.

"Dad, did you want to talk to me?" Jake asked.

"Yes, we do. Come into the house; your mother and I want to ask you something."

Vinci got a huge smile on her face.

Jake looked at Vinci. "Do you know what they want?"

"No idea," Vinci said with a straight face.

"Hey, buddy, will you have a seat?" Dan asked.

Jake and Vinci sat down with their mom and dad.

"So, Jake, what are you doing tomorrow?"

"It's Saturday. I don't know … hopefully run my Big Wheel in the driveway," he said as he looked out the window, wondering if the weather was going to cooperate.

"Oh, we have something better to do than run the wheels off the Big Wheel. Would you like to go to the MRP Go-Kart store in Three Oaks and buy a *race-ready high-performance go-kart* tomorrow?" Dan asked Jake.

Dan and Julia were sitting on the edges of their seats, waiting to see Jake's reaction.

"Do you mean it? You're not kidding, are you?" He rose up out of his chair with pure excitement, realizing that his dream was about to come true.

"No, we're not kidding. Your dad was over there looking at the karts, and he likes what they have to offer," Julia said with mixed emotions. She was worried whether he was going to be okay.

"Yes! Yes! Yes!" Jake said, pumping both fists in the air. "I would love to go tomorrow."

Vinci laughed when she saw her brother's reaction to the news, but deep down inside, she felt a little jealous.

"Okay, then. Tomorrow we will go!" Dan said enthusiastically.

2

Fulfilling the Plan

The next day, the whole family got into their SUV and drove over to Three Oaks to the MRP Go-Kart Shop. When Jake walked inside the shop, he was amazed by the karts; they were low profile, sleek, and red.

"Wow, Dad, these karts are cool!" Jake said.

The shop owner, Tony, came from the back room and greeted the family. "Welcome back, Dan. This must be the family, and this must be the seven-year-old you were talking about."

"Yes, this is my wife, Julia, and my daughter, Vinci, and, yes, this is my son, Jake, whom I told you about."

"Well, Dan, what can I do for you today?"

"Well, we want to purchase a kart for Jake today."

Jake had the biggest smile on his face.

"The young lad is excited, I see. Okay, let's get him started," Tony said.

Jake slowly walked over to the karts and looked over each one without saying anything, yet his family could see the excitement in his body language. He then swiftly moved through the karts, looking them over and then looking up at his mom and dad, grinning. "I can't believe this! It feels like I'm dreaming," said Jake. "Vinci, will you slap me so I know I'm not dreaming?"

Without any thought, Vinci walked over to Jake and pulled back her hand.

Julia grabbed Vinci's hand as it was swinging forward. "Vinci, you know better. Jake was just kidding," she said.

Vinci pinched her lips together and raised her nose with frustration because of all the attention he was getting.

Jake spotted a kart that looked like he could fit into it. "I like this one," he said.

"That's a good choice and a great starter kart for your age," Tony said.

Jake got fitted into his racing go-kart, the smallest of the karts. It had a nine-horsepower engine with a maximum speed of thirty-five miles per hour. Jake was beaming as he sat in the seat, while Tony adjusted the seat position for him. Tony grabbed the smallest helmet he could find. The color was red.

"Perfect! I love that color," Jake said. The helmet fit snug, perfectly around his head, covering his chin, only leaving a small opening around his eyes to see through. His racing suit fit him comfortably. He could move his arms and legs in different directions. Jake stood there proudly for the first time by his racing go-kart while wearing his racing suit and helmet. You couldn't see Jake's face under his helmet, but if you could imagine a seven-year-old boy for the first time getting what he'd been dreaming about, you would see complete happiness and excitement! His beaming eyes under the helmet told the story!

"*Wow*! Look at you! You look like a hot-shot race car driver," said Dan.

Julia and Dan had their cell phones out, taking pictures of Jake, seeing him for the first time in his complete racing gear.

"Would you like to use the track today? The first lesson will be free, and we can get you completely set up," Tony said.

"Yes, that's what we want to do. Get us set up. I have a trailer that we brought with us so we can load the kart up and follow you to the track," said Dan.

Jake was taking the suit and helmet off while Dan and Tony were talking. He said to his mom and Vinci, "I cannot wait for my first run on the track. I've dreamed about this day for a long time, and now it's here!"

On the way to the racetrack, Jake was talking up a storm. His parents weren't surprised about his excitement. And Vinci tried to comment on his conversation, but she could not get two words in.

Arriving at the racetrack, Jake was looking out the SUV window and was amazed by the track. They all got out of the vehicle and walked over to Tony. He started to explain to them about how to get through the gate with the combination and where everything was located on the property.

"Are you ready to get started?" Tony asked Jake.

"You bet I am," Jake replied.

"How often will we have to change the tires?" Dan asked Tony.

"Not often, these are not a soft tire, so you can get a lot of miles out of them. Okay, Jake and Dan, this is where you start the kart, and here is the choke. These are the gauges to your speed and fuel, and here is your oil pressure gauge."

"Is this going to be okay? I'm a little worried," Julia said.

"We're going to be with you guys whenever you need us, and Jake will do fine. Don't worry," Tony said as he put his hand on Julia's shoulder. "Everyone say hi to Steve. He is one of my assistants here. What we're going to do is get one of our karts out of the garage, and Steve is going drive the kart while Jake follows his line, learning how to go into and out of the corner and accelerate successfully without wrecking," Tony said.

"Yes, you were mentioning that back at the shop, about getting power as you come out of the corner," Dan said.

"Yes, and Jake will learn all that today. Okay, Jake, are you ready?" Tony asked.

"You bet. Let's go!"

Jake stepped into the kart. He was very nervous, hoping that he would be able to drive it well and thinking it was much different from his Big Wheel at home.

He put on his helmet.He took his right finger and clicked on the power button. With his left hand, he pressed the start engine button. After listening to the engine start for the first time, he pressed on the gas pedal and listened to the engine rev up.

"Sounds good," Jake said to Tony and his dad.

"Okay, Jake, can you hear me?" Tony said, talking through his headset to Jake.

"I sure can, Tony," Jake said, anxiously waiting.

"How about you, Steve? Can you hear me?" Tony said.

"Loud and clear, Tony," said Steve.

"Okay, Jake, this is not a race. This is about you getting familiar with the kart, so follow Steve and stay on his line; stay one kart length back, and do exactly what he does. Also, you will need to listen to me. I will be coaching from the side of the track," said Tony.

"Okay, I will," said Jake.

"All right, Steve, let's start out with a moderate speed until Jake gets comfortable with the kart."

"You got it, Tony."

Jake pressed the gas pedal, lightly at first. His hands shook on the wheel, and Jake thought to himself, *I can do this.* He sped up to catch Steve, following right behind him.

The karts swerved back and forth to let him get the feel of steering, punching the gas pedal, and absorbing the takeoff. They went into the first turn, and Steve took a wide sweep and then cut the corner very tightly and powered out of it with good acceleration. Jake was one kart length back, doing exactly what Tony told him to do.

"Very good, Jake. Stay with him," Tony said through his headset.

They went into the second turn, doing the same thing. Their speed got up to fifteen miles per hour as they drove down the front straightaway.

"Well, Jake, how do you like it?" Tony asked.

"I'm ready for lap two," said Jake.

"Yes, you are. You handled that first lap like you know what you're doing. It's like you have been driving for a long time. Let's turn it up, Steve. Do the same thing again. Jake, stay with Steve only one kart length back," Tony said.

"Okay, Tony," Jake said.

Jake knew the speed was going to pick up, so he wrapped his fingers around the steering wheel, squeezed the wheel, and then released it. His eyes were focused like a tiger's when ready to strike its prey.

Steve and Jake came up to the front straightaway. Steve put the pedal down, and the karts got up to twenty-five miles per hour. This time, Jake was right on Steve's bumper.

***

"What is Jake doing out there?" Dan said, with a worried look on his face.

Tony took his headset off, looked at Dan and Julia very seriously, and said, "You guys have something special here. I have been doing this for forty-five years and have never seen anybody take a liking to a kart as fast as Jake has. He is at the level five right now; at that level, a driver has been racing for three years. Everything he is doing—the handling, the acceleration, the precise turning—is a level five entry. When a new student follows Steve for the first time, they stay at least four kart lengths back. They never keep up with his speed. We ask them to stay one kart length back, but they never do. And now Jake is following Steve, right on his bumper. This comes with practice, skill, and total concentration of the driver. And that is level ten driving."

He put his headset back on and said, "Keep doing that, Jake. Stay on his bumper if you're comfortable with it."

"You mean to tell me that this is not beginner's luck?" Dan said.

"You can't have beginner's luck in racing. You might follow the driver for thirty seconds, but you're going to crash because of the speed. You will get nervous as to how fast you are going and crash. Not Jake, though, he is right on Steve's tail, and he's not letting up," Tony said.

Tony spoke to Jake again. "Okay, Jake, if you think you can pass Steve, go ahead and do it, but don't wreck him."

"Okay, Tony, let's see if Steve can keep up with me," Jake said, smiling widely.

"I'm ready, Jake. Let's race!" said Steve.

They crossed the start/finish line, and both karts opened up, topped out running at a speed of thirty-five miles per hour. Jake was right on Steve's bumper. They went into turn 1. Steve went wide and cut into the corner. Jake stayed high and passed Steve coming out of the turn. He took the lead.

"Way to go, Jake! You are driving with authority," Tony said.

Going into turn 2, Jake took the corner wide and then cut in tight through the turn. Steve stayed with him but not close enough to pass. Jake raced through the S curves, taking the corners tight and accelerating out of the turn. They came up to turn 3, the tightest turn of them all, and Jake sped up.

"You need to take this turn a little slower, Jake! Slow down before you wreck!" Tony screamed very nervously.

Jake did not listen. Instead, he kept his speed up and powered the kart around the corner. His back end started to slide around. He then accelerated to make up for the back end sliding. The tires grabbed traction and slung him through the corner, leaving Steve way behind him.

"This is unbelievable! The last time I saw a move like that was many years ago. I was very young—just starting out here when a young lad by the name of Joe Pearson did a move just exactly like that!" said Tony.

Dan and Julia looked at each other and could not believe what Tony had just said.

"You want us to keep racing?" Jake asked.

"A couple more laps. You're looking good, Jake. Keep it up," said Tony. "What's going on, Steve? Can't you catch him?"

"I'm giving it everything I got," said Steve.

"What was that driver's name? The one who made that move just like Jake did?" asked Dan.

"Joe Pearson. He was pretty talented behind the wheel. He even holds some records at M-40 Speedway's track. I doubt if they will ever get beaten," Tony said.

Julia and Dan looked at each other really strangely after Tony's comment, and Dan thought, *Maybe this is meant to be*, and possibly that his father, Joe, had something to do with it.

"All right, guys, bring the karts in," said Tony.

"I didn't have to coach Jake that much. You sure he never raced before?"

"The only racing he's done was in the playground at his school, where they had a footrace," Julia said.

"And some in the driveway with his Big Wheel," Dan said.

"This kid is a natural," Tony said, shaking his head.

"He appears to be just like his grandfather," Dan said.

"Oh, yeah? Who was that?" Tony asked.

"Joe Pearson," said Dan, looking at Tony and understanding where his talent was coming from.

"No way," said Tony.

"Yep, our last name is Pearson, and my dad did race at M-40 Speedway, although he never talked about racing out here. I'm sure he raced at a lot of places I never knew about," Dan said.

Tony looked at Dan, puzzled.

"Do you guys want to go out for some lunch? My treat," Tony asked.

"Sounds good. I am starving," Julia said.

"Me too," said Vinci.

"Great! Let's go to Redamak's. They have the best burgers. Let's lock up the karts in the barn," Tony said.

The Pearsons loaded into their SUV and followed Tony to Redamak's restaurant in New Buffalo, Michigan. It was about a fifteen-minute ride to get to their destination, but it seemed like only two minutes because of the excitement they all shared about Jake's performance on the racetrack.

When arriving at Redamak's, they got out of the SUV. They were still chatting up a storm about Jake's performance. They walked into the restaurant with Tony, and the waitress seated them and took their drink orders.

"Have you guys ever been here?" Tony asked.

"Yes, we have. It's one of our favorite places," Dan said.

"You know, Jake is a gifted driver, as I mentioned at the track. In time, I could see him entering into some races. You and the family can start out by going to the track as often as you can. Get a lot of practice time in for Jake. Racing with more than one person is different, and it requires some practice. We can set up some pretend races with other drivers, and everyone benefits from it. Does that sound like something you all would like to do?" Tony asked.

"Absolutely, that sounds like a great plan," Dan commented.

"First off, the safety needs to be taken seriously! Watching Jake drive thirty-five miles per hour scared the daylights out of me. I was not expecting to see that kind of driving from him," Julia commented.

"Yes, I totally agree with that," said Dan.

"That's our first objective, safety. We are all about that, as you'll soon see," said Tony.

"I hope so because you telling Jake to pass Steve made me really nervous. I don't think that's being safe. It's his first time driving," said Julia.

"Julia, like I mentioned before, I recognized Jake's talent immediately, so you're going to need to trust me in my decision making with him. There will be a time when he will move up to a bigger kart with more horsepower, and you're going to have to trust me when I say it's time. The last thing I ever want is Jake to be hurt!" said Tony.

Jake and his sister sat there quietly, listening to the conversation between them. The food was brought in, and everyone enjoyed eating their world-famous burgers.

"So, Joe Pearson is your dad, huh?" Tony asked Dan, looking at him with a puzzled look.

"Yep, I did not know much about his racing career. It took a turn when he could not feed his family on the sport. He went to work in the factory and gave it up totally."

"That's too bad because he was a talented driver," said Tony.

Jake and Vinci decided to act up in the restaurant with french fries hanging out of their noses and making pig noises, making everybody laugh at them.

"You guys are goofy! We're going to leave you two here!" Julia said.

"Well, I think we should be going," Dan said.

"Okay, you guys," Tony said. He grabbed the tab from Dan. "You need to be quicker than that!"

"You don't need to do that."

"I want to! And I will see you guys real soon. Here is a key to get the kart unlocked from the barn."

"Thank you, Tony, and, yes, we will see you soon."

***

Over the following year, Jake's newly discovered talents never ceased to amaze his parents and sister. After a lot of practice and wrecking two karts, he was at the point of almost quitting, yet he couldn't because he felt an outside force pushing him to succeed. Jake felt a connection to Mike McConnell. Every once in a while, in his dreams, Jake experienced death flashes from beyond as Mike's last moments flashed through his mind. He moved up to a bigger kart, a twenty-nine-horsepower engine with a top speed of fifty miles per hour.

It was now summertime, and Jake and Vinci were on a school break. Dan and Julia were confident that it was time for Jake to start racing at the local track, and Jake couldn't be more excited for it.

3

The Time Has Arrived

The Pearsons showed up at the MRP racetrack at 4:30 on the dot. There were already people there setting their karts up. The first thing they did was look up Tony.

"Over here, Pearsons," Tony said, waving his arm really high. He was at the fuel station, putting fuel into his racing cans.

"Okay, guys, are you ready for this?" Tony asked.

"Yes, Jake is definitely ready. That's all he's been talking about since lunch," Dan said.

"Good, this will be very exciting for you, Jake. You will always remember your first race. Okay, let's get over to the barn and get the kart out. You're going to want to use a higher octane, which will increase the horsepower; everybody uses it when they race. The first can is on the house."

"Wow, I really appreciate this, Tony," Dan said.

"No problem," he said as he was unlocking the barn.

Tony and Dan pulled the kart out of the barn and gave it a good look-over. "The first thing we do is go over to the booth to get a racing number and register for the race."

"Hey, Jake, do you want to go with us?" Dan asked.

"Where are you going?"

"To register and get you a racing number."

"Cool! Yeah, I will come. Can I have number 9, Dad?"

"They give you numbers on availability. Depends if they have it," Tony said.

"What is so special about number 9?"

"That was Mike McConnell's number."

They got to the booth. Tony helped Dan register for the first time. While Dan was registering Jake for the race, he asked the attendant if his son could have number 9 for his kart. Number 9 was still available. Jake got the biggest smile on his face.

"You will be qualifying third, so you will want your kart lined up and ready to go around four fifty-five," the attendant said.

"Okay, no problem," said Dan.

"All right, we need to go back to the kart and get you set up. Jake, why don't you get your racing suit and your shoes on?" Tony asked.

"That's a big ten-four, good buddy!" Jake pointed his finger at him.

Tony kind of tilted his head with a puzzled look on his face. "Your grandfather always said that," Tony said.

"No way," said Jake.

"Yeah way," Tony said with great enthusiasm.

"Okay, Dan, you want to place your numbers on the front right here and on the side over there," Tony said. "This sticker is officially kart approved. You never want to take this sticker off. But take off your racing numbers because you might have a different number next time," Tony said.

"Okay, got it," Dan said.

"Now check the air pressure in the tires and the lug nuts on the wheels. After that, drain the fuel out of the gas tank and replace it with the higher-octane fuel. This stuff is expensive, so only use this when you're racing. That's pretty simple, huh?" Tony asked.

"Yeah, that's easy enough," said Dan.

"Okay, let's get lined up. Jake, bring your helmet with you," said Tony.

"Yeah, get lined up," Jake said while he helped push the kart over to the line.

Jake sat in his kart and waited for his turn to qualify. While waiting, he watched the first kart take to the track and take off. It had good speed and qualified in 34.29 seconds.

The second kart took to the track at 34.27 seconds.

Jake was told to bring his kart onto the track and get ready to start his qualifying lap. Jake looked around and absorbed everything. He noticed a very tall, slender man walking alongside the track. The man had on a racing outfit. It looked to be very old and out of style. He walked with his arms swinging at his sides and a long-legged stride. The man looked at Jake, smiled, and gave him a thumbs-up as he kept walking. Then the man just faded away into the sun. Jake squinted his eyes to see if he could see him anymore, but the man was gone.

"Okay, number 9, you're up. When that light turns green, you start. Any questions?" the track attendant asked.

Jake squeezed the steering wheel and put his game face on. "No, I'm ready."

The light turned green, and Jake put the pedal to the metal. He came up to turn 1, driving the high side and cut low into the corner while accelerating through the whole turn. He slung himself down the straightaway to gain speed. Coming up to turn 2, he drove high and then dropped low into the turn. He accelerated through the turn to help him stay tight through the corner. He sped through the S curves very fast. Coming up to turn 3, the tightest turn of them all, Jake did his power brake slide again, and then he slingshot himself through the corner of turn 3, speeding down the front straightaway at fifty miles per hour and passing the finish line at a time of 29.16.

"Wow, that was amazing, Jake! You have just broken the track's time trial record. The record before was 30.12 seconds by Joe Pearson, your grandfather. It took many years for somebody to beat that record, and then it was done by his grandson. This is unbelievable," replied Tony.

"You're kidding me, right? Nobody has beaten that time until now? After all these years and all this new technology?" Dan asked.

"Your dad was an amazing driver. He could drive a tin can the speed of these new karts any day! There was no driver like him until now."

Jake drove off the track and pulled his kart around where his parents were. They were all excited about his time.

"Way to go, son. That was some good driving out there," Dan said.

"Yeah, buddy. Way to go out there," Julia said, hugging him.

"You were smoking up the track," said Vinci.

"Yeah, and it felt good too," Jake said.

The rest of the karts qualified. There were a total of ten karts racing that night. Jake had the pole position.

"Will all the racers please report to the track and line up your karts in the order you qualified?" the track announcer said.

"Well, buddy, this is it. Keep your headset on so we can communicate through the race. You have thirty laps. Take it easy, and have fun," Dan said.

"Okay, Dad."

"Do good out there, buddy, and be careful!" Julia said, giving Jake a big hug.

"I will, Mom.""You go, Jake," Vinci said.

"Okay, Sis."

"Have fun out there, Jake; you already have the lead," Tony said with a smile.

Jake laughed. "You're right, Tony."

All the karts lined up in their qualifying order, and the racers stood beside their karts, listening to the national anthem. Each had his right hand placed on his heart. After the national anthem, the racers got into their karts and waited for the announcement.

"Gentlemen, start your engines!" the announcer said.

Jake took his right hand and turned on the power, using his left hand to press the start engine button. The engine started with one press of the button. The nine other drivers fired up their engines. The smell of the high-performance fuel lingered in the air. The twenty-nine horsepower engines had a high-pitched revving sound. Jake could feel the vibration of the other karts behind him when they were revving up their engines. He'd never felt that before, and it was a little intimidating to him. His body temperature rose another five degrees. Even though it was a cool evening in Michigan, to him, it felt like it was extremely hot. In front of him was a man holding a green flag. Behind the man was the sun, facing the drivers and blinding them a little. Jake pulled down the tinted shield on his helmet so he could race straight into the sun.

"Okay, Jake, when the light in front of you turns green, start racing. There will also be a guy waving the green flag. In case you miss the light, you'll see the flag waving. Good luck and race hard," Tony said.

"Okay, I will."

The light turned green, and the flagman waved the green flag.

"Go, Jake, go!" Dan yelled.

Jake put the gas pedal down and got a jump on everybody else. He came up to turn 1 going high, and he dropped down low at the turn. He powered through the turn and accelerated up to turn 2. Going high again, Jake dropped into the turn and then powered out of the turn and raced through the S curves, staying tight all the way through. He came out of them and slowed down for turn 3. He cut the corner very tight and then accelerated out of the turn, racing down the front straightaway and passing the start/finish line.

"That's lap one. You have twenty-nine more. You're looking good out there. Your lap time was 31.27; keep it up!" Tony said.

Dan was watching Tony and learning. He knew that he would be coaching Jake for the next race.

"The second-place kart ran a time of 31.32 seconds," Tony said.

"Okay," Jake said very quietly.

"You can tell he's very focused on what he's doing," Dan said.

Jake's eyes were fixed on the race as his hands lightly held the steering wheel. He was gracefully running the fast line, and his body was really leaning into the turns.

Two men walked up to Tony and Dan, very interested to see who was racing in the front kart. Their names were Mike Johnson and John Stevens. Their sons were also racing.

"Hey, Tony, how's it going?" Mike asked.

"It's going good, Mike. How about you?" Tony asked.

"It's going good, also."

"Hi, John," Tony said.

"Hi, Tony. Who is that out there racing in the lead kart?" John asked.

"His name is Jake Pearson, Joe Pearson's grandson."

"Really? How long has he been racing?" Mike asked Tony.

"A little over a year," Tony said with a big grin.

"You're kidding me! That kid out there has to have been racing for at least four years or better," Mike said.

"Nope, Jake has been practicing a lot, but this is his actual first race," Dan said.

"Mike and John, this is Jake's father, Dan Pearson."

"Pleasure to meet you," Mike said.

"Yeah, nice to meet you and welcome to racing," John said.

"Thank you."

Jake had raced fifteen laps and managed to keep the competition behind him as he started to lap karts.

He then caught up with the last kart following him through the S curves, going through turn 3. Jake was right on the number 6 kart's bumper coming out of the turn. He made a quick pass, accelerating up to fifty miles per hour, leaving the kart way back.

Jake went into turn 1. He passed a kart on the high side and powered around him like his competition was sitting still.

Jake continued to methodically work himself through the race, passing six karts down one lap.

"Has he said anything to you, Dan?" Julia asked.

"No, he has been focused on the race. It's amazing he has not let up through the whole race, constantly charging through the pack. I just can't believe what I'm seeing, and neither can anybody else! He has found his calling," Dan said.

"Okay, Jake, five laps left. You have pushed really hard. Now just follow the race; don't pass anybody else," Tony said.

"Ah, Tony, I'm having fun. I don't want to follow anybody," Jake said.

Tony laughed and shook his head. "Go ahead and finish it out your way."

"Thanks, Tony," Jake said.

Jake put the pedal to the metal and really pushed through the race, making his last five laps an average time of 30.27 seconds.

"Last lap, buddy," Dan said.

Jake went through the corners like he had been doing except for turn 3, when he did his power slide move. All the spectators were amazed by his driving ability.

Jake powered down the front straightaway at a high speed, putting his left hand in the air at the waving checkered flag.

"Way to go, buddy. You've won! You did it," Dan said.

"Nice driving out there today," Tony said. "Make a victory lap, and wave at everybody," Tony said.

"I would be glad to."

"Then bring your kart over to Victory Lane."

Jake made his victory lap and did a couple of doughnuts in front of the start/finish line. Then he drove over to Victory Lane.

He parked his kart in Victory Lane and then turned off the engine. He stood up in the kart and put both fists in the air, hooting and hollering.

Everybody in Victory Lane cheered and applauded with excitement. Jake's mom, dad, and sister ran up and gave him a big hug.

"We're so proud of you," Julia said with a big smile.

"Way to go, brother," Vinci said.

Jake's dad gave him a high five. "Way to go!"

Tony came over with a trophy and said, "Jake, it's an honor to give you this trophy tonight. You raced with courage, concentration, and commitment. It sure was a pleasure watching you tonight. You have what it takes to be a champion, and we look forward to seeing you around here for many more races."

Jake reached his hands out, as Tony handed him the trophy. "It's been a wonderful day today. I have dreamed about this day for a long time. Thank you, Mom and Dad, for buying me this racing kart."

"Can you guys come over to the garage for a minute before you leave?" Tony asked the Pearsons.

"Sure, Tony, we can do that," Dan said.

Julia nodded.

"Jake, would you drive your kart over to the garage?" Dan asked.

"Okay, Dad."

"There is something I would like to show you. Here's the schedule for this year's season at this track and also at the Indiana track. I thought you might want to know the upcoming events," Tony said.

"What are those, Tony?" Jake asked, pointing at some magazines.

"They're some old magazines from past races in the Winston Cup series. Would you like to have some?"

"You bet I would. Thank you."

"Okay, Tony, this schedule will be helpful for us, and I really appreciate everything you've done for us. I told Julia the first time I met you I had a good feeling about your company. I think we will be out here this week for some practice and probably will be here at least three times a week. Jake is looking forward to more races, aren't you, Jake?"

"You bet I am!"

Tony laughed. "You guys have had one heck of a day. You need to get home and kick your feet up."

"I agree. Let's get packed up," Julia said.

"Okay, the boss has spoken. Let's get moving," Dan said.

The whole family cracked up laughing. Julia and Vinci started loading their stuff into their SUV while Dan and Jake got the kart loaded into the trailer. Then they packed up and headed for home. When they got home, the family unpacked everything. Dan and Jake put the kart away in the garage, and they both stood there and stared at the high-performance racing machine. Dan shook his head and smiled.

"Hey, buddy, where is your trophy?"

"Oh, it's still in the SUV."

"Let's take it into the house and put it in a special place."

"Okay," Jake said with a big smile.

Dan and Jake went into the house and found the girls.

"Hey, where do you think a good place would be for Jake's trophy?" Dan asked.

"How about over here on top of the fireplace mantel?" Julia replied.

"Yeah, that's a good place."

"Hey, would you like a fire in the fireplace tonight?" Dan asked Julia.

"Great idea. Would you guys like some popcorn to go with the fire?" Julia asked the kids.

"All right!" everybody said.

Dan started a fire in the fireplace, and Julia popped a big bowl of popcorn. The Pearson family got cozy around the fire in a big blanket.

Dan had the bowl sitting on his lap with Julia snuggled beside him. Vinci was snuggled close to her mom, and Jake was snuggled close to his dad as they gazed into the fire.

"Hey, Dad," Jake said.

"Yeah, buddy?"

"When I was getting ready to qualify, I saw somebody walking along the side of the racetrack. He had a racing uniform on, and he was looking at me as he walked. He smiled at me and gave me a thumbs-up. Then he just vanished into the sun," Jake said.

"Do you know who he was? Have you ever seen him before?" Dan asked.

"When we were in the SUV going home, I was looking at the magazines Tony gave me, and I saw he was in there."

"Who was it, honey?" Julia asked Jake.

Jake reached over and grabbed the magazine that was lying by the couch. He opened the page to the person he had seen.

"This is the guy I saw today," Jake said as he pointed in the magazine.

"Jake, this picture says it is Bo Anderson, three-time Winston Cup champion, and the teenager standing by him is his son Colt Anderson, who won the Winston Cup two times. Jake, I don't think Bo is alive anymore; his son Colt is in his late sixties or early seventies by now," Dan said.

"No, this guy looks exactly like him. A young man, not an old man!"

"This picture was taken a long time ago when Colt was a teenager. It says here he was sixteen years old, so his dad was probably in his thirties or early forties."

"He was even wearing the same racing suit! I know that was him."

The girls were eating their popcorn and listening to them argue. Then Julia joined in the conversation.

"Okay, Dan, what if it was him? It's possible that Bo Anderson could have been there. After all, who would have thought that Jake could drive as well as he does? Doesn't that seem a little strange?" asked Julia.

"You know, you're right. This all seemed to start when Jake asked about Mike McConnell."

"Yes, and that afternoon, he was racing with his friends around the playground, remember?"

"You're right," Dan agreed.

"I am just doing what feels right, Mom and Dad," Jake said.

"Of course you are. We believe you, Jake. If you said you saw Bo Anderson, then we believe you did," Julia said.

Dan agreed with Julia. "Yes, we believe you, buddy," he said as he gave Jake a big hug.

"Mom and Dad, I'm tired. Can I go to bed?" Vinci asked.

"I think we all should," Julia replied.

Everybody got ready for bed while Dan went into a trance watching the fire go down in the fireplace. Eventually, he fell asleep and dreamed about the man Jake was talking about, Bo Anderson

***

He was young and looked tall and slender with a nice smile. He also had that old-style racing uniform that fit him very tight. They were standing in the middle of a racetrack in Jones, Michigan. Up on a billboard was the name M-40 Speedway. The billboard changed to a movie screen, showing fast images of Jake growing older and progressing in the sport of racing.

Bo said to Dan, "Jake needs your support all the way to the end."

Dan looked up at the billboard and saw Jake in a fiery kart wreck.

Dan lurched awake from his deep sleep. His clothes were wet from sweating. He lay still on the couch and thought about the dream, fighting his inner conflict over his burgeoning fear for Jake's life. The fire was burned out, and everybody had been in bed for a couple of hours. Dan rubbed his arm from the chill and thought back on the dream. "All the way to the end." *What does that mean?* he wondered. He then made his way up to the bedroom and cuddled up to Julia for the night.

***

The following morning, Jake walked to the door that led to the garage and opened it slowly with his eyes closed. When the door was opened wide, he opened his eyes and looked into the garage to see a red Birel racing kart sitting there. "Good, it was not a dream," he said with a big smile.

He went into the garage and started rubbing off the dirty spots that were showing on the kart, while he recalled the day he'd had yesterday. Sitting in the driver's seat and wrapping his fingers around the steering wheel, Jake glared at the garage door and started having a vision of Mike McConnell racing at Darlington Speedway. He saw him with his helmet on, racing hard around the track. He could only see his eyes and hands and where he was driving. Then the vision was gone. Jake shook his head, "What was that?"

Dan stared at Jake. "Who are you talking to, son?"

Jake turned his head to the door really quickly. "You scared me, Dad!"

Dan laughed. "I thought I would find you out here."

"Yeah, I just wanted to make sure it wasn't a dream."

"Yeah, I felt the same way, son. What a day you had! May there be many more."

"Yeah, I hope so."

"There will be. You're just getting started. Let's talk about this more over breakfast." Dan put his arm around Jake. "I'll race you," he said.

They both took off running through the garage and into the kitchen. All the rustling around woke up Julia and Vinci.

"What are you guys doing?" Julia asked.

"Dad's making breakfast. Would you like some?" Jake asked his mom and Vinci.

"No, I just want to go back to sleep," Vinci said, upset.

"I would love some," Julia said as she sat down at the table to visit with the guys.

The Pearsons enjoyed their great breakfast together, telling jokes and making fun of some of the people they'd seen at the racetrack the previous day.

Later that morning, Dan drove up to Pine Edge golf course, where he worked. He visited with the employees and the golfers. Dan's friend, Jeff Michaels, was standing in the clubhouse, looking at a new set of golf clubs.

Jeff owned a grocery store in Cassopolis, Michigan, and he was also a racing fan at M-40 Speedway. He had been going out there for years. Once in a while, they would rent the party deck, break out the margarita machine, and party like there was no tomorrow.

Dan walked over to Jeff and struck up a conversation with him about the M-40 Speedway.

"New owners took over. That makes the fifth owner since it was built. Nobody understands why someone would put a million-dollar racetrack out in the middle of nowhere."

"Maybe, it was a special spirit that drew the first owners to build it, and maybe that spirit is finding people to keep it open?"

"You could be right," Jeff said.

"I didn't know you followed racing, Dan. I knew your father had some racing records there." He continued, "You never wanted anything to do with it. Why the change?"

"My son, Jake, has taken an interest in it, so I bought him a racing kart. You know I have to tell you that we are having fun with it."

"That's great! You know, we should take Jake over to the track to watch some racing. I know the owners personally. They actually put your dad's racing records on a beautiful display for everybody to see. And he still holds those records to this day."

"Really, we should. How about this Friday?" Dan asked Jeff.

Jeff nodded. "Sounds good to me. Why don't you meet me at the store around five o'clock?"

"Okay. Jake will be excited!"

Dan wrapped up what he needed at the golf course. He headed home to enjoy the rest of the day with his family. When he got home, he told Jake the news about that Friday. Jake was very excited. He couldn't wait to watch some late-model racing.

"Is that all right with you, Julia, if we meet Jeff at his store and drive up to Jones and watch some racing?" asked Dan.

"Yeah, that's fine. Vinci and I will do some clothes shopping."

"Yeah, let's do that, Mom!"

"Are you sure you're okay with that?" Dan asked Julia again.

"Yes, of course! You guys will have fun."

"Thank you, honey." Dan kissed his wife. "Let's go to Lake Michigan and have a picnic today," he said.

"Yes, that's a great idea!"

Everybody agreed.

They enjoyed the rest of the day at Warren Dunes State Park. The Pearsons had their cookout, enjoyed the lake, and did some dune climbing.

The weekdays were very busy. Jake was at the Rolling Green Raceway Park, sharpening his driving skills Monday, Wednesday, and Thursday from 6:00 to 8:00 p.m., while Vinci was at her dance practice on Tuesday and Wednesday from 5:00 to 7:00 p.m. Dan took Jake to the racetrack while Julia took Vinci to dance practice.

4

A Visit from the Past

Dan was talking to Jake and Jeff as they were driving to the M-40 Speedway.

"Friday couldn't come quick enough! That's all I've been thinking about since we talked at the golf course," Dan mentioned to Jeff.

"I know, right!" Jeff struck up a conversation about the racetrack. "Have you guys ever been to this track?"

"No, this will be the first time for Jake and me," said Dan. "I always wanted to. Then, when I decided to, I talked myself out of it."

"Well, the new owners have done a nice job honoring your father," added Jeff.

"Yeah, how is that?"

"They've displayed a memorial of his racing career. It shows pictures of him and the records he has broken. It's really impressive."

"It's going to feel very strange going to this place."

"Isn't it time to see your father's accomplishments?"

Dan nodded.

Jeff, Dan, and Jake arrived at the track with time to spare before the first race started.

The racetrack sat in an open field about two hundred yards off the highway. You could not see the racetrack from the parking lot because of the enormous stadium seating that circled the track. The evening was calm and still. A beautiful full moon added light to the evening's race. The temperature was in the high seventies so they didn't need a jacket to keep the chill off their bones. They could see the lights turning on, getting ready for the evening race.

Dan was sitting in the SUV, quietly staring at the track. He felt sad for his dad, because he could not live out his dream of racing. Instead, he chose to work in a factory full-time, and on the weekends, he stocked shelves in a local grocery store to feed his family. Dan rarely saw him growing up, but when he did see him, he was angry and resentful toward him and his family. Dan ended up moving out on his eighteenth birthday, and that was the last time they talked before he passed away.

They stepped out of the SUV. Dan took a deep breath and then exhaled. Both of his hands were squeezed into fists. He then opened his fingers, stretching them. "Well, what are we waiting for? Let's go and have some fun," Dan said.

"Yeah, let's go, Dad!"

Jeff nodded, agreeing with Dan. They walked to the ticket booth, paid for their entries, and went inside.

Once they were inside, Dan saw a huge concession stand. Past the concession stand on a grassy surface were some picnic tables. The outside area was very clean. There was no trash on the ground. The whole place was painted up with a red-and-white design. There were kids running around with huge smiles on their faces. It was like being at the local fair, except for there were no rides. They walked under what seemed to be a bridge but actually was the announcer's booth. Under the booth was a lot of information about the driver's seasons. Over to the right was the display of Dan's father's racing records. What a proud but sad moment Dan shared with his son.

Staring at his racing records, Dan felt very proud of his dad but sad because he was not able to enjoy that time with him. Dan grabbed Jake, held him very close, took a deep breath, and said, "Look at all these records he's got out here. He was a hero out here. No wonder he grew very angry when he gave up what he loved doing."

Jake grabbed his dad's hand. "You know, I don't think he is angry at you. He just didn't have a great dad to help him like you're helping me. And I think he would be proud of you."

Dan inhaled deeply and wiped the tears from his eyes. "Oh God, look at me." He was very embarrassed.

Jake looked up at him with very loving eyes. "Don't be embarrassed." He squeezed his dad's hand again. "It's okay."

Jeff put his hand on Dan's shoulder. "Yeah, it's okay."

Dan shook his head, tightened his lips, squinted his eyes, and said to Jeff, "You're right; they did a beautiful job honoring him."

Then he turned and looked at Jeff, placed his hand on Jake's head, and said, "Well, are you guys ready?" with a half-crooked smile.

Jake looked at his dad and said, "If you are."

"Okay, let's go watch some racing!"

Dan got control of his emotions. It wasn't easy. Feelings about his father, confusing and painful, still swirled around as he headed toward the stands with Jake and Jeff. Just then, he heard a voice calling out to Jeff. A short, bald man with a beard approached, his hand extended in friendship. Jeff introduced the man as the owner of the track, and Keith Herman offered to let them all watch the races from the announcer's booth.

***

They got up to the booth, looked out the announcer's window, and saw the entire racetrack. Keith was very excited to learn that the legendary Joe Pearson's family was with him that night. Everybody got comfortable in some reclining chairs; they also helped themselves to refreshments in the refrigerator.

"So, Dan, you must have been at this track many times," stated Keith.

"No, not really. This is my first time here actually. My dad did not take us to the track, unfortunately."

"Wow, that is unfortunate!"

"I must say, you did a beautiful job displaying my dad's racing records."

"Why, thank you. That was all Dee's doing."

"Who is Dee?" Dan asked.

"Dee is my wife. Here she comes now."

Dee rushed into the announcer's booth. She extended her hand and greeted everyone.

"Sorry, I am really late!" she said.

"She does this all the time. I can set my watch by her!"

The guys all cracked up laughing.

Dee sat down in her usual chair. She grabbed the microphone and started talking to the fans.

"Welcome, race fans, to the beautiful M-40 Speedway. We have a warm, beautiful night. Tonight, we're going to have late-model racing, five-heat, ten-lap races. After a short break, we will have a one-hundred-lap late-model race. The winner takes home ten thousand dollars."

The crowd cheered very loudly.

Keith jumped into the other announcer's chair, grabbed the other microphone, and said, "Let's have the first heat of cars at the starting line, please."

Six cars lined up for the first race, according to their qualifying order. They pulled up to the start/finish line, turned their engines off, and got out of their cars. The national anthem played; they all faced the American flag with hands on their hearts. After the national anthem, Keith grabbed the microphone and told the racers to get into their cars and wait for the announcement to start their engines.

***

Since this was Jake's first time seeing the big cars race, he was taking it all in and very excited about being there.

Keith turned and faced Jake. He asked, "Would you like to make the announcement?"

"What announcement?" Jake asked.

"Gentlemen, start your engines," Keith replied.

Jake got the biggest smile on his face. "Why, sure!" He beamed.

Jake grabbed the microphone with his right hand, put it close to his mouth, and said loudly, "Gentlemen, start your engines!" After Jake made the announcement, he listened to the engines start. He was very impressed with the loud sound the late-model cars made.

He scanned the cars and noticed, standing in the back of the racetrack, Bo Anderson.He was wearing the same racing outfit he had been when Jake saw him at the Rolling Green Raceway. Bo looked up at Jake and gave him the thumbs-up.

"Dad, come over here."

Dan walked over to the window. "Yeah, son?"

"Do you see that?"

"What am I looking at?"

"He's here!"

"Who's here?"

Jake whispered into his dad's ear, "Bo Anderson."

"Where do you see him?" Dan asked very quietly.

"Over there by the wall." Jake was pointing.

"I don't see him." Dan focused his eyes, trying to see.

"He just waved at me." Jake pointed over by the wall again. "I think he wants to talk to us," he whispered.

"Are you sure, Jake? I don't see anybody where you're pointing."

"There! He's doing it again."

"Let's walk over there," Dan replied.

"Where are you guys going?" Jeff asked.

"Just for a walk. We will be right back," said Dan.

Dan and Jake walked out of the announcer's booth, down the stairs, past the concession stand, to the back of the racetrack.

"There he is, Dad!"

Over by the wall stood a tall, slender man, wearing an old-fashioned racing suit.

"Holy crap, I can see him!" said Dan.

"I told you, Dad!"

Dan and Jake walked up to Bo Anderson very hesitantly.

"It's a nice night for racing," said Bo.

"Uh-huh," they said, with puzzled looks on their faces.

"Jake, I saw you racing the other day. You looked really good."

Jake looked at his dad. "I told you it was him!"

Bo smiled. "Dan, did you think about what I told you?"

"Yes, you told me to support Jake all the way to the end. I am not sure what that means, but I heard you."

Bo smiled again. "You have a very talented son who will be able to do some incredible things really soon. Until then, you support him on what journey he chooses. He will know instinctively what path to choose."

"Always will," Dan said.

"I have to go. I need to get ready for a race." He then winked and smiled at Dan and Jake.

"Oh, would you mind opening the gate and letting me out?" Bo was looking at Jake.

"No, I don't mind." Jake grabbed the gate, pulled it open, and watched Bo walk into the open field toward the woods. When he got to the woods, he turned and waved at them. He took a couple of steps into the woods and started to vanish. Then, he was gone.

Jake and Dan looked at each other; they could not believe what had just happened.

"Jake, I think you need to close the gate before somebody yells at us."

Jake smiled and pulled the gate closed.

"Let's get back before Jeff wonders where we are," Dan said.

"All right, Dad."

Dan and Jake walked back to the announcer's booth and sat down in their chairs. Keith and Dee were having a good time announcing the race. They even let Jeff do some announcing.

"About time you guys came back. We missed you," Dee said.

"We were just taking a tour around the place," Dan said.

"Is that why you had the gate open? You wanted to see what the woods looked like?" Keith asked with a smile.

"Yeah, we wanted to see how big the property was," Jake said with a smirk on his face.

"You got back just in time. The next race will be the one-hundred-lap, after a short break," Jeff said.

"Cool," said Jake.

Dee stepped out of the announcer's booth for a minute. When she got back, she handed Dan a picture of his father that came from the display.

"I thought you might want this."

"Why, thank you very much." Dan was very choked up about Dee's kindness.

"I understand. That was his first win here."

Keith picked up the microphone and announced the one-hundred-lap race would be starting in two minutes.

"Let's have the cars line up in their qualifying order and get this race started!"

After the cars got lined up, Keith looked at Jake. He asked him, "Would you like to make the announcement again?"

"Why, sure I would." Jake grabbed the microphone and yelled loudly, "Gentlemen, start your engines!" The crowd cheered. Jake was still amazed by the awesome rumbling noise the cars put out.

The late-model cars made two slow laps around the track. When they saw the green flag, they increased their speeds up to 150 miles per hour. They slowed down through the corners to a speed of 120 miles per hour. The whole place shook. Jake looked at his dad and Jeff. They had big smiles on their faces.

"*This is so great!*" Jake said, screaming to be heard over the loud engines.

They all smiled and nodded, agreeing with Jake.

The one hundred laps went by too quickly. The winner that night was a racer out of Buchanan, Michigan—Tony Nichols.

Dan and Jake were so grateful for the hospitality they had received from Keith and Dee. "You guys need to come back really soon," Keith said.

"We will, and maybe we can get Jake out here racing in a few years," Dan said.

"Yes!" Jake said, pumping his fist.

"All right, it would be great having another Pearson out here breaking records," Keith said.

"He has already broken his grandfather's racing record at the Rolling Green Raceway in Buchanan."

"Really? He's held records over there this long?" Keith asked.

"It took his grandson to break them. Impressive!" Dee said with a smirk on her face.

"Yeah, it was a shock to us too," replied Dan.

"Come on out anytime," said Keith.

"We will. Thank you again for everything," said Dan.

Dan, Jake, and Jeff loaded into their vehicle and headed home for the night.

Jake looked out the window into the darkness of the country road leading from the track toward home. It had been a great night, but he was tired. He was glad when his dad dropped Jeff off. He couldn't get home to bed soon enough.

"Hey, Dad?" he asked, looking over at his father.

"What, son?"

"How is it that we can see dead people?"

5

Staying Cool and Focused

Jake felt a wave of anxiety wash over him at the sight of the immense track. He'd seen others in the several previous months at races in surrounding states but nothing like this one for the big July Fourth event. As he watched the crowds filling the seats, he thought back. "Wow, Dad! This is one big track," Jake said, shaking his head.

Tony grinned. "You bet it is! And I've got a good feeling about this one. Don't wanna jinx it, but …"

"Why haven't we ever raced at this track since it's so close?" Jake asked his dad.

"I don't know. We just got busy racing in other states."

Tony brought a map of the track. He placed his arm around Jake's shoulder. "Jake, look here at the front straightaway. It's a lot longer than the Rolling Green Raceway's. Turn 1 is very narrow, just like the last turn on the RGR track."

"Yeah, it is."

"And then turn 2 is very wide. Turn 3 is tighter than 1. Four, five, and six are S curves. Then you have a straightaway off of six. Then it goes into a big S curve, starting with seven, and finishes out in turn 10 as you race past the start/finish line. Take this map, look it over, study the turns, and when it's time, you won't have any problems."

"Okay, thank you, Tony."

Jake was studying every turn and every degree. As he was studying the map, he slipped into an altered state. The noise of the track suddenly faded away. His vision narrowed, almost as if he were in a tunnel of light with darkness all around. "Jake?" a voice called. He looked around but didn't see anyone. It was Mike McConnell. He was getting ready for a race. Mike was studying a map at Dover International Speedway, the monster mile. Mike was wearing mirrored sunglasses. When he looked up from the map, he could see the reflection of the monster mile in his shades.

Jake then lost the vision, shook his head, and said, "Whoa! What was that all about?" He was confused by what he had just seen. He went back to try studying the map, but he could no longer concentrate because of the distraction he had just had.

***

All the top drivers were showing up at the track. The past champions from Europe were trying to get a win and get back into the racing circuit. Last year's champion was there, hoping to continue his success.

"Wow, Dad, look at their expensive equipment!" Jake said.

"Don't let that bother you, buddy," his dad replied.

"Yeah, Jake. None of those drivers have the heart that you have," Tony commented.

Jake clinched his jaw and stared down last year's champion.

"Don't let him get to you, Jake," Tony said.

"I can see his soul. He is scared of me." Jake continued to intimidate him.

"You're having fun with this, aren't you, buddy?" his dad asked.

Jake turned his back to the champion. He looked at his dad, winked, and smiled.

Dan started laughing. "What do you mean, 'I can see his soul'? You crack me up."

Tony, Jake, and Dan laughed hysterically.

"Let's get the kart ready for qualifying," Dan said.

"Sounds good," said Jake.

Tony agreed with them.

They walked over to the check-in and registered for the race. Jake was able to get the number 9 again. He also drew the twentieth position for qualifying.

"Have your kart lined up for qualifying when the eighteenth-position kart starts qualifying," said the registration person.

"We have some time before we qualify," said Dan.

"That's okay. We can go over the kart thoroughly," said Tony.

***

Dan, Tony, and Jake got the kart out of the Featherlight trailer, along with their tools, tent canopy, and lawn chairs.

They started setting up the kart for the race, changing over the gasoline, and doing their normal checkups.

As they were going over the kart, Tony saw a small hairline crack on the engine block.

"Oh boy. Look at this!"

"What is it, Tony?" asked Dan.

"Oil is leaking off the motorhead. You have a hairline crack!"

"If Jake tried qualifying, he could possibly make the crack larger, lose compression, and not make it in the top thirty."

"This isn't good," Dan commented.

"I have a motor back in Three Oaks. We need to get it before his time is up for qualifying."

"Let's go then!" said Dan.

"Stay here. We don't have time to pack up. You can take the motor off so when I get back, it won't take long to put the new one on."

"Sounds like a plan." Tony got into Dan's vehicle and drove off very fast.

"Boy, I hope he makes it back in enough time," said Jake.

"He will," said Dan. Dan looked at Jake pretty nervously. "I never took off a motor before."

"It's okay, Dad. We will do it together." Jake knelt down and looked the motor over.

"Right here are the bolts that hold the engine to the kart. And here is where we need to disconnect the chain from the back sprocket to the front sprocket. And this is the throttle cable that gets disconnected from the engine."

Dan was amazed how racing and mechanics came so naturally to him. *How could this be?* he wondered. "How do you know all this?" asked Dan.

Jake smiled. "I don't know. I just do."

The two of them had the motor off the kart in forty-five minutes.

"Wow, Jake, we're good!" Dan looked at his watch. "Tony should be arriving at the shop any minute; we're going to make it in time, buddy. Don't worry."

The announcers made an announcement. "The first five karts need to line up for qualifying," he continued. "The qualifying will start in fifteen minutes."

Dan's eyes got really big. "This will be close, buddy. You're going to need to keep your cool."

"I will try, Dad."

Tony called Dan on his cell phone. "I got the motor; I'm on US12, pushing it hard to get back on time."

"Good, Tony, because qualifying will be starting in ten minutes."

Tony inhaled really deeply. "All right. I am hurrying."

"Be careful," said Dan.

"I will," he said.

Jake and Dan took a walk over to watch the first kart qualify. It was the previous champion from last year, Jack Johnson.

***

The light turned green, and he put the pedal to the metal. Jack took a quick glance at Jake and then turned his focus back to racing. He came up to turn 1, slowed down through the turn, and accelerated out of it to turn 2. He slowed down through turn 3, accelerated up to turn 4, and sped through turns 5 and 6. He went through turns 7, 8, and 9 really fast. At turn 10, he accelerated through the turn to the start/finish line, finishing with a time of 42.762 seconds—a new track record.

Jack jumped out of his kart and pumped his fist, looking at Jake, trying to intimidate him.

Jake turned his back to him and said to his dad, "Great, that's all I need is for him to break the track record!" He continued, "I got my work cut out for me today."

"You know what, buddy? If there's anybody who can beat him, it will be you." He continued, "Don't let him get to you. All he's trying to do is needlework you."

"You mean, treat me like a pin cushion and stick needles in me?"

"Exactly. Don't be the pin cushion. Ignore him."

"What? I don't see anything! What just happened?" Then Jake smiled at his dad.

Dan smiled back at him. "Exactly! Let's go back to the kart."

"Sounds good. I will race you back!"

Before Jake could get all the words out, Dan was already running. "Hey, wait up, you cheater!"

Dan had a three-step lead on Jake. When they got back to the kart, Jake was the winner.

"Good race." Dan put his right hand in the air and gave Jake a high five.

"Good race," Jake replied.

Julia and Vinci came driving up. "Hey, how are you guys?" Julia asked.

Dan and Jake looked down at the kart. "We've got some challenges ahead of us," replied Dan.

"I can see. Why is the engine off the kart?"

"There's a hairline crack in the engine block. It's leaking oil. Tony drove to Three Oaks to get another one," replied Jake.

"Can we have drivers five through ten line up their karts for qualifying?" the announcer asked.

Jake placed his hands on his head. "Man, I hope he hurries up." Just when Jake said that, Tony came pulling in. "Yes, he's here!" Jake said with excitement.

Tony slammed on the brakes and jumped out of the vehicle. "We need to move fast, guys!"

Dan opened the back end of the SUV. Tony ran up to help pull the engine out.

"Let's put it down right here for now," said Tony.

"You guys did a nice job, taking out the old engine," Tony commented.

"Can we have karts 11 through 16 lined up for qualifying?" the announcer asked.

"Oh boy." Tony took a deep breath. "We're going to do this in record time!" They set the engine on the kart and started bolting it down to the frame. Jake handed Tony the chain to be attached to the sprockets.

"Why don't you get suited up, buddy?" Dan asked Jake.

"Okay, Dad."

Tony and Dan were moving very fast to get the kart set up. Finally, they got it all together. Tony tried starting it, but it would not fire up.

"Can we have karts 17 through 20 lined up for qualifying?" asked the announcer.

"It's okay. We have until the eighteenth kart gets on the track. Then, we have to be up there," said Dan.

Jake walked up and checked the kart out.

"The fuel line is not attached," he said.

Tony looked at it. "By golly, you're right. I can't believe I missed that." Tony got the fuel line hooked up and started it up on the first pull. Jake put on his helmet and drove over to the lineup.

"Just in time, buddy. Stay focused and drive hard," said Dan.

"Okay, Dad. I just wish I could have practiced."

"You don't need to. You're the best!"

Jake nodded and gave a half-crooked smile.

It was now Jake's turn to qualify. He pulled up to the start/finish line and waited. The light turned green.

Jake put the pedal to the metal. He came up to turn 1 and sped through the corner, only slowing down a little bit. He raced up to turn 2, sliding the back end. He tapped on the brake, slowing down to the tightest corner, turn 3. He raced up to turn 4 and then sped through turns 4, 5, and 6. He then raced down the straightway to turn 7 and leaned really hard into the corner, getting the maximum speed that he could get. He raced through turns 8 and 9, the same way he did on turn 7. Coming up to turn 10, he lost power. The kart started to slow down.

"Jake, why are you slowing down?" asked his dad.

"There's something wrong with the kart. I barely have any speed."

The engine shut down. He coasted across the start/finish line with a time of 49.52 seconds.

Jake got out of his kart very discouraged with the time. He looked over at Jack Johnson and saw that he had a huge grin on his face. Dan and Tony came running up to the kart.

"What went wrong, Jake?" asked Dan.

Tony looked at the engine and saw bubbles coming out of the fuel line.

"Look! The fuel line has a hole in it."

"It's okay, Jake. We'll be all right," Dan said, giving him a hug on his shoulder.

The track announcer walked over to them. He said, "I've never seen anybody run as fast as Jake did. Too bad he had to finish with kart problems. On the bright side, he will still probably qualify in the top thirty because of the good run."

Dan, Jake, and Tony were very excited when they heard that news.

"Let's get this kart back to our area so we can work on it," said Dan.

They pushed the kart back to their pit area and started to work on the broken fuel line. Tony had the fuel line replaced. The kart tuned up and was running very rich.

"Wow, Tony, the kart sounds very good!" Jake commented.

"I gave it every inch of horsepower I could get out of it."

"We can tell. Sounds like the kart is ready for a long race," Dan replied.

An announcement was made for all the drivers: "Please come over to the start/finish line to check the boards to see if you qualified and also check your pole position."

Jake, Dan, Tony, Julia, and Vinci went over to see the starting positions.

"Look, guys. I made it! Thirtieth position!"

"All right! Way to go!"

Dan and Julia hugged Jake.

"This will be my first time starting from the back. I'm kind of looking forward to it."

"That's the right attitude, buddy," said Julia.

"Yeah, Jake, you're going to put a hurting on those guys!" Vinci commented.

"There will be a short meeting in ten minutes at Victory Hall for all the drivers. After the meeting, the race will start," the announcer said.

All the drivers gathered in Victory Hall to hear the rules of the race. Once they got all the information, they went back to their areas. They had thirty minutes to gather all their stuff, get a quick snack, and line up their karts for the race.

The karts were all lined up two by two. The national anthem was sung. The drivers got into their karts, waiting for the announcement to get started. The stands were filled with spectators. The air had the aroma of fair food—cotton candy and brats. Young kids were playing on the grass hills, pushing and rolling down them.

"Gentlemen, start your engines!" the track announcer said.

The karts all started at once. The horsepower from the engines revved up loudly. Jake's engine had a distinctly different sound. His kart sounded more powerful than all the other karts.

They made three laps around the track before the green flag was waved. Drivers were coming up to the final lap on turn 10. The karts were revving up for the green flag to wave.

The flag was waved, and the race was on. Jack Johnson got a jump out in front of everybody.

Jake was back in the thirtieth position, feeling frustrated because of the slow karts in front of him.

"Take it easy, Jake. It's a long race. You will have to make your way to the front one kart at a time. We have plenty of time," said Dan through his VHF radio headset.

"Okay, Dad."

Twenty laps into the race, Jake had passed ten karts. He was now running twentieth.

"You are passing a kart every two laps, and you are running in twentieth position. We've got plenty of time to get to the front. Keep up the good work."

"I am having a lot of fun back here, Dad. The kart is running strong. I could really open it up and pass a lot of karts, but I'd rather save that until the end."

"Good idea."

Jack Johnson continued to run very strong up front, not letting anybody pass him. On lap 40, he blocked a kart from passing him and wrecked him into the wall, causing a caution flag to come out.

At that time, all the karts made their first pit stop. The karts drove down pit row in a single file line, each kart pulled into its pit. When they got to their spots, it was a quick fill up in the gas tank and back out on the track. Jake picked up three positions from the quick pit stop. He was now running in the seventeenth position. All the karts were back on the track in a double-row restart. They had followed the pace kart for two laps.

"Okay, Jake, we are on lap 43. Continue to run cautiously and make your way to the front," Dan said.

"Okay, Dad. I can't wait until I'm up front, racing against Jack Johnson!"

"It'll be here sooner than you think!"

The green flag was waved. The karts were racing again. Jake got beside kart 43, and 07. They were running three-wide down the front straightaway. Jake had the inside lane coming up to turn 1. Kart 43 was wedged in the middle. Kart 43 bumped 07 on the side and pushed him off the track. Jake sped up to get in front of them.

"Whew! That was a close one, buddy!"

"I know. That was scary."

"Take it easy. You are now in the fifteenth position."

"Okay, Dad, I will pass one kart per lap." Jake continued to methodically move his way to the front. On lap 57, he moved into second place.

"All right, Jake. You are now following Jack Johnson. Follow him for three laps, size him up, and try to find his weak spot. Then make your move."

"Sweet. This is going to be fun," Jake commented.

Jake gave Jack a couple of bumps from the back, just to let him know he was there.

Jack swerved back and forth to keep Jake from passing.

"You got him nervous, buddy!"

"I know. He is driving careless."

Jake got beside him down the straightaway. Jack got nervous and bumped into the side of Jake.

"Whoa! This guy is an idiot, and he's making me mad!"

"Be cool. That's what he wants you to do—get rattled."

"I know, Dad. I got something for him, though."

Jake continued to follow Jack, giving him pressure. He was having fun trying to rattle him.

"We are going to need to pit again, Jake."

"I know, Dad. When do you want me to?"

"Let's wait for Jack to pit first."

Just as Dan said that, Jack pulled into pit row. Jake followed him, along with the rest of the karts. They topped off with gasoline, and back on the track, they went. Jake was still in second place.

"Okay, Jake, you're on lap 75. Now is the time to start thinking what you're going to do," Dan said.

"No worries, Dad. I already have a plan!"

The karts followed the pace kart for two laps. The green flag was waved, and the race was back on.

On lap 80, Jake and Jack were approaching turn 2. Jake did his famous power-slide trick around Jack. He slingshot around the outside, passing him for the lead.

"No!" yelled Jack, while pounding his fist on the steering wheel.

"Good job, Jake! Now let's put some distance between you and him," Dan said.

Jake put the pedal down and started setting speed records. Jack never had a chance to catch him.

The crowd was totally amazed by his power-slide trick and the dominance he had on the racetrack.

"Okay, Jake, last lap. Let's make it a good one," Dan commented.

"No problem."

By now, Jake was twenty-five seconds ahead of Jack Johnson and was starting to lap karts.

Jake sped through the start/finish line. He saw the checkered flag and put both fists in the air!

"You did it! Way to go! You're the best!" Dan shouted.

"Whoa, I can't believe this. What a day! We did it!" Jake replied.

After a long and exhausting race and all the hard work he'd put in on the tracks, he felt very rewarded and proud of himself. His parents hugged him after the victory, and he felt the love and excitement from them. And Jake knew that the connection he had with Mike McConnell had something to do with him winning.

He bent down, picked up the whole trophy, and raised it over his head, smiling ear to ear.

The president of the Birel racing team walked over to congratulate him. He then gave Jake his contract for the upcoming year.

"Take a couple of days to look the contract over, and then give me a call. We'll set up a time so we can sit down and sign the papers together."

"Okay, sir," Jake said with a big smile.

6

The Ending of My Past Life

Jake felt another spasm in his stomach. It was even more painful than the last one. His dad pulled into a rest stop, said they should all take a last bathroom break, and got out of the car. Despite his pain, Jake was excited. He could hardly believe it had been three years since that first day he'd driven on Tony's track. And now he was a national champion in his class and age grouping.

"What's wrong, Jake? You don't look well," Julia said.

"I don't feel so good," he said, holding his stomach.

"Let me check your temperature." Julia got into the suitcase and found a thermometer. She then took Jake's temperature.

"You are not running a temperature, and your color looks fine."

"I don't know, Mom. I never felt like this."

"Well, why don't you sit back, lie down, and rest."

"All right," he said and moaned.

Dan and Vinci jumped back into the vehicle. "Is everybody ready?" Dan asked, as he looked back into the SUV. "What's wrong with Jake?" he asked Julia.

"I don't know. He's not feeling well," she said.

"Hang in there, buddy. We're almost there."

"Okay, Dad," said Jake, holding his stomach.

Dan placed the keys into the ignition, started the SUV, and put the vehicle into drive. They were back on the road again, driving through Wilkesboro. When driving through the city, they came upon an old racetrack that had been closed down since 1996. Jake stood up from his seat and screamed, "*Stop! Stop* the vehicle right now!"

Dan slammed on his brakes. The car behind him almost hit the back end of the SUV. The other cars were putting on their horns and the drivers yelling, "Why don't you learn how to drive, you darned Yankee?"

He then pulled off to the side of the road, stopped the vehicle, and turned around. He looked at Jake and said, "What is your problem?"

Jake's eyes were really *huge*. He grabbed the door handle, opened the car door, and jumped out of the vehicle. Just as his feet hit the road, a speeding car flew by him. The car slammed on its horn and swerved, trying to avoid hitting him.

Jake's mom screamed, "Look out!" as she grabbed the dashboard.

***

Jake ran up to the old abandoned racetrack, put his hands on the fence, and tried looking inside. Dan, Julia, and Vinci ran up to Jake. They were very upset with him.

"You almost got killed back there, young man," Dan said with a worried look on his face.

Julia grabbed Jake's arms, knelt down, and looked him right in the face. "What is going on, Jake? Why did you just run across the road and put your life on the line?"

He pointed at the racetrack with a distressed look on his face. "I need to get inside there."

"Why, Jake? The place is closed up. We can't go in there," said Dan, very frustrated with him.

Jake started climbing the fence.

Dan pulled on his pants. "Get back here. What is wrong with you?"

Jake got very frustrated with them. "Dad, you don't understand. I need to go inside there."

"Why? Give me one good reason."

Jake stared at his dad for a long time, trying to come up with the right words. It seemed like an eternity.

"Jake, answer your dad. Why do you need to go in there?" Julia asked.

Jake's lips tightened up together. He started chewing on his bottom lip because he was nervous.

"Okay, I will tell you. There is no other way except for telling you straight out. I need to go in there because it is the ending of my past life," Jake said with authority.

Dan and Julia were shocked by his comment. They stood there as white as ghosts, not sure what to say.

"Jake, honey, I know we have been experiencing some abnormal behavior from you, but this is over the top! I'm freaking out right now! I don't know what to say," Julia commented.

Dan was studying Jake's face. He had never looked so intense. He could see the urgency on his face.

"Honey, I think we should go in there and find out what's troubling him," he said.

Julia looked at Dan with a stunned expression on her face. She thought maybe there were two crazy people now.

"Look, he is very bothered with this. We need to go in there with him and figure this out," said Dan.

Julia took a good look at Jake and realized what Dan was saying. "Okay, Jake, let's find an opening because I am not scaling a fence," she said.

They walked around and found a hole cut out in the fence by a previous trespasser. The fence hole was approximately three feet in circumference, just enough space for somebody to squeeze through.

"If we get caught, we're going to jail," Vinci said.

"Be quiet," Jake said.

Vinci gave Jake a mean look. "You be quiet!"

Everybody squeezed through the small fence hole. The last one through was Dan; he got his new golf jacket caught on a wire dangling from the fence opening.

"Come on, Dan. What are you waiting for?" asked Julia.

"Yeah, hurry up, Dad," said the kids.

He tugged on it for a minute, getting frustrated with everybody rushing him. He finally pulled on it, tearing a big hole in it. "Ah, man! I hope they are happy now. This is my brand-new jacket," he mumbled to himself, very frustrated at his new rip. He finally made it through the opening.

Julia looked at the rip. "Aww, I am so sorry, Dan. I think I can fix that."

"Don't worry about it. We need to get moving before somebody sees us. I have taken up too much time here."

Jake wasn't saying anything. He had a catlike air to him. His fingertips were in his pockets, and his eyes were focused on every little detail. His shoulders were hunched over, and his walk was slow, as if he were channeling some outer force.

Julia noticed a sign that was in the middle of the racetrack. It read, "Winston Cup Series." Below the sign, on a big pole, were the numbers 1 through 10, which kept track of what place the drivers were in.

"Look at all those bleachers," Vinci said.

"Look at how big the announcer's booth is. This track was made to accommodate a lot of people," Dan said.

There was wear and the old-age decay the racetrack had accumulated. There were cracks in the cement where weeds were growing through. On turn 3, written on the safety wall, were the words "North Wilkesboro Speedway." On turn 1 was a sign that said, "Junior Johnson Grandstand."

"This old racetrack has had the best of the best race here—Bo Anderson, Colt Anderson, Junior Johnson, Richard Petty. And the last one who won here was Jeff Gordon in 1996," commented Jake.

Jake walked over to the start/finish line. He was still in that catlike mode. His parents and Vinci were behind him, walking very slowly and listening to every word he was saying. "Here is where Darrell Waltrip beat me by a half of a second in 1989. We battled all day long, and at the end of the day, I gained his respect. And over here on turn 1, Colt Anderson ran me into the wall on the final lap, causing me to blow a back tire and lose the race."

"So you're saying you were here before? Do you remember who you were?" asked Julia.

Before Jake could answer his mom, an old man came out from nowhere. He startled the Pearsons.

"Don't be alarmed," he said in a southern accent. He stood five foot nine, with shiny gray hair; he used a walking cane to help himself get around. Jake walked up to the old man and stared at him for a few minutes. He felt like he knew him or had seen him before. He grabbed the old man's hand and gently held it. He closed his eyes and started remembering who the man was.

"Steven Webster, that's your name. You are the owner of this place," he said with excitement.

Steven nodded and said very quietly with a tear in his eye, "You remembered."

"I do! We were best friends; we spent a lot of time on this racetrack."

Dan and his family stood there with their mouths open wide, listening to their conversation.

Steven extended his hand to Dan. "Hi, I'm Steven Webster."

Dan put his hand out and shook Steven's hand. "Yeah, I heard," he said.

"I'm very sorry. This must all be a shock to you," said Steven.

Julia extended her hand. "Hi, I'm Julia. Yes, it is a shock."

Steven nodded, agreeing with her. "Why don't we all go back to my house, put on some coffee, and start from the beginning."

"Good idea. Just like the good old days," Jake said.

Dan and Julia stood there in shock. They could not believe what they were hearing. They followed them across the racetrack, listening to their conversation about the good old days.

When they got to turn 2, Jake stopped walking. He stood and stared at the wall for a good two minutes, remembering his accident.

"I can remember that I was frustrated. How loose the car was handling. I hit the wall going 180 miles per hour. I don't remember anything after that." Jake stood there as white as a ghost. "Here is where I died, isn't it, Steven?"

"No, that is where you wrecked! You died at the hospital," he said.

"Jake, do you remember your name then?" Julia asked again.

"I do remember. I was Mike McConnell, the four-time Winston Cup champion."

Jake's parents' mouths dropped to the ground.

"How could this be?" Julia asked.

Steven continued, "I was told that when Mike McConnell died, his spirit floated outside the hospital. A spirit eagle put him on his wing. They traveled to a small town called Buchanan. A new baby was traveling home from the hospital. That baby was Jake. The eagle tipped its wing and watched Mike's spirit fall right into Jake's body."

Dan and Julia were shocked by what they had just heard. Julia gently grabbed Jake and pulled him in close to them. She was holding him ever so tightly.

"And who told you this?" Dan asked.

"Bo Anderson."

"Of course. It all makes sense now. When he talked to us at the M-40 Speedway, he said Jake would do some incredible things really soon." He continued, "He would instinctively know what path to choose."

"Yeah, Bo is a very special spirit. Other people can see and talk to him. Not all spirits can do that. Some spirits need a little extra help."

"What do you mean by 'a little extra help'?" Dan asked with an inquisitive look on his face.

"You'll see. Let's go back to my house and finish talking there."

"We have so much to ask," commented Julia.

"No problem. All your questions will be answered."

"Hey, Jake, do you remember which way to go?" Steven asked.

"Yeah, over there through that fence, down the asphalt path."

Steven laughed. "Yep, you're right."

They got to Steven's house. He fumbled around for his keys.

"Here, let me help you," Dan offered.

"Thank you," said Steven.

Everybody followed him into the house. He was walking in slowly. The house was very dark, and the shades were closed. There was a smell to the house, as if it had not been cleaned in a long time.

"Can we open up some of the shades?" Julia asked.

"Sure, go ahead. It's been a long time since the sun has shined in here."

Julia lifted the shades. They could see an inch of dust all over everything. Hanging on the walls were pictures of past race car drivers who raced at North Wilkesboro Speedway.

"Wow, look at all these pictures," Vinci said.

"Are all these pictures from your racetrack?" asked Julia as she looked very closely at each one of them.

"Yes, all the best raced here," said Steven. "Neil Bonnett, Red Byron, Bobby Isaac, Leeroy Yarbrough, Glen Wood, Herb Thomas, Fireball Roberts, Marshall Teague, Curtis Turner, Joe Weatherly, Tiny Lund, Fred Lorenzen, Cotton Owens. That's just a few of the names on the wall."

"Oh my, Dan. It's your dad," Julia said.

"What? That's impossible," he said.

"No, his name is even under the picture. It is your dad."

Dan walked over and looked at the picture. It was from 1962, right before he was born. Dan looked at Steven. "Did you know my father?"

"Yes, I did. He raced here only once. But he made a big impression on everybody; the trophy shows for it."

Julia handed Dan the picture. He dusted it off clean. Then he grabbed it with both hands and looked at it very closely. He was lost for words. He wished he had known his father better. He struggled with the fact he treated his dad poorly. Dan finally understood that his dad had loved him and showed it with all the hard work he did to feed his family. He felt really bad and wished he could take it all back—leaving the house and never speaking to him again. He placed the picture close to his heart. "I miss you, Dad," he said, squeezing the picture very tightly.

"He came down with a friend. His name was Doug VonKoenig, a real hot shot from the North. Doug ended up getting ill from food poisoning, so Joe Pearson drove for him. The biggest promoters tried following him after the race. Nobody could seem to locate him. It was like he quit racing altogether," said Steven.

"He did practically. I guess he found out I was on the way so he decided to get a real job. He did a few races here or there, but that's about it," Dan said.

"That's a shame because he had talent," said Steven.

"Yeah, he basically stayed at one track, M-40 Speedway. He still has a lot of unbroken records there," said Jake.

"Well, all of this has to be overwhelming for you guys."

"Yes, it is. We found out that our oldest kid has Mike McConnell's spirit in him and my dad was one heck of a racer. Yeah, I'd say it's a little overwhelming," said Dan. "Reincarnation. I never gave it a thought. How does this work? Does Jake have his own spirit? And, yes, I am actually overwhelmed, too. It seems like this was all planned out from the beginning."

Steven smiled. "This is no coincidence. Jake does have his own spirit; he also has Mike McConnell's spirit, and he will not stay with him forever. Sometimes a spirit is not ready to pass on to the other side, for one reason or another," he continued. "So Mike made a spiritual decision to stay here. The spirit eagle chose Jake for reasons we don't know. I will tell you what I do know. Jake has the ability to let other spirits come back, and that's why he is here."

"What! How can he let other spirits come back?" Dan asked.

"Since Jake has Mike's spirit in him and his own spirit, they are equally united to form a bond that gives him the ability to let other spirits come back, just by opening the gate for them."

"What gate?" Jake asked.

"The gate inside the racetrack that leads to the outside wooded area. Once you place your hand on that gate and open that door, your spirits within you will open a new dimension. A door for them to travel back through."

"Well, let's go do it!" said Jake very excitedly.

"No, Jake, we have to get ready for them."

"What do you mean get ready for them?" Julia asked.

"The spirits that will be coming back are the past NASCAR greats. We need to get some race cars here and have the racetrack fixed up so they can race again. There is no way they can race on that old, cracked-up, weed-infested racetrack," said Steven.

"You're saying that they will be able to race cars? And physically drive them on this property?" asked Dan, very confused.

"That's what I have been told," replied Steven.

"And who told you that? Let me guess—Bo Anderson?" replied Dan.

"Yes, it was he who told me," commented Steven.

"That's going to take a lot of money," said Julia.

"Yes, it is, but when they come back, people will pay to see their past heroes race again."

"You mean to tell me that other people will be able to see them?" Julia asked.

"Oh, yeah. And they will drive from far away to come and watch them race. And they will fill the stands every night. People will feel good again, watching their heroes back on the racetrack. Once this place is cleaned up, we can open the gate and let them relive their dreams." There was a quiet stillness in the air after Steven was done talking.

Dan was very inspired by his speech. "I say we start cleaning this place up."

"What? We have jobs, commitments, race schedules, and school. We can't do this. And where is the money going to come from?" Julia asked.

"From our savings."

"Our savings? Are you crazy? What if these spirits don't come back? Then what? And did you forget we signed a contract with Birel racing? They are expecting us to be there. They won't let us out of that."

"Come on, Mom. We need to do this," said Jake.

Julia saw everybody staring at her, waiting for a decision. She felt pressure from the family.

"It's going to take a lot of work to fix this dump." Julia was concerned about everything that could go wrong, and she was concerned that Dan was reacting too fast, not thinking through everything clearly. But she knew that if she did not go along, they would never forgive her.

"All right, Dan, let's do this. But I am concerned about it."

"You won't be fooled, Julia. You're making a good decision," said Steven as he placed his arm around her shoulder.

"I hope you're right," Julia said very quietly under her breath.

"Steven, I know where we can get some race cars. We have some friends up north, Keith and Dee Herman. They are the owners of the M-40 Speedway. I'll call them and ask for their help," said Dan.

"Great. And I know a cement company that will reseal this track," said Steven.

"And we can put some fresh paint on this place, too," Julia contributed.

"Well, let's start making some calls and get busy. I am anxious to see some ghosts race on this track," Dan said.

7

Sprucing Up the Old Place

Dan, Julia, Jake, and Vinci were in the SUV on the way into town to buy paint and other supplies. Steven warned them about how nosy they could be in town so they were to try not to look so conspicuous.

The family was really quiet on the drive into town. Each of them was taking in everything that had happened—especially Dan. He was struggling to believe what he was doing, even though he knew it was foolish. But perhaps he was doing this because he wanted to see Joe again to resolve the conflict that remained unresolved between them.

Upon arriving at the hardware store, Dan turned off the vehicle and sat quietly staring out at the store. Julia asked him if he was okay. Dan nodded and asked Julia, "The ghost that Steven mentioned, do you think …" He stopped himself, thought about what he was going to say for a few seconds, and then changed his mind.

"Never mind. Let's go inside and get some paint," said Dan.

Inside, the store was your typical hardware store. A few employees were working. They were very helpful.

"Excuse me. Are you new in town? Did you just move here?" one of the locals asked the Pearsons.

"Yes, we are new here," Dan replied.

"We're fixing up the racetrack," Vinci said with a big smile.

"What racetrack? Wilkesboro?" one of the locals asked, butting into the conversation.

"Yes, Wilkesboro," Dan said.

"Why would you be doing that? That place has been closed for eight years," the owner of the hardware store asked.

"We just feel like painting, so what other place needs it more than Wilkesboro?" Julia said with a funny expression on her face.

The owner and the other locals looked at the Pearsons as if they were crazy.

"Well, I think this is all we need for right now," Dan commented.

The Pearsons paid for their supplies and left as fast as they could.

When they got back to the racetrack, they were cracking up. They were trying to explain to Steven how everybody was acting in the hardware store. They found it hilarious.

"Don't let them bother you. They mean no harm," said Steven.

"It's just funny. Why do they have to know our business?" asked Julia.

"Those guys are crazy. Heck, they will probably be going really bonkers when they see the cement trucks rolling in," said Steven.

"Yeah. I bet they will probably call the local news station, too," said Jake.

Everybody cracked up laughing for a long time.

"Well, Steven, we're going to go check into a local hotel. We will be back in the morning," said Dan.

"What? You guys can stay here; you don't need to stay at a hotel."

"Are you sure? We don't want to put you out."

"Heavens no. The company will be nice for a change."

"Okay, then, we will stay here."

"Good, the concrete will be getting delivered Monday morning, and we can start tomorrow morning cleaning this place up. It will be good to have you close by," said Steven.

Dan called Keith Herman from Steven's house and told him what was going on. He left out some of the details, but Keith agreed to send down twelve late-model race cars. He said they would be arriving on Sunday. He and Dee would be personally bringing them down. Steven was excited about the good news. He could finally see the picture coming together.

"I have waited a long time for this day to come."

Dan placed his hand on his shoulder. "We're going to make this place look brand new for the boys."

"That would be great," Steven said with a smile.

***

Evening time came. The Pearsons were sitting around a fire that Dan had built in the fireplace. Steven got to talking about the past. He was trying to see how much Jake really remembered.

"We had the best races here. People would fill the stands on a Sunday afternoon. They would drive from three states away to catch the hottest and fastest drivers on the racing circuit. You could smell the hot grills cooking their favorite food."

"And I remember the intensity waiting for the race to start. On a hot summer day, you would sweat waiting for the green flag to wave. And I would drink a gallon of water to keep from dehydrating," said Jake.

"You do remember," said Steven.

"I remember racing against Jeff Gordon, Mark Martin, and Bobby Labonte here. They were my friends and competitors. And I remember how the track conditions would change after racing one hundred laps and how we would have to adjust our tire pressure to compensate for the change. I remember that this five-eighths mile speedway has an uphill/downhill effect on the straightaways. One straight banked slightly upward; the other banked slightly down. And I also remember in the seventies, Cale Yarborough dominated at this racetrack."

A low-light fire was burning. Dan was intensely listening to Jake and Steven. Dan asked the question about his father. "Do you remember anything else about my dad?" he asked Steven.

"No, Dan, nothing I haven't told you already. You were not kidding about not knowing that he raced here?"

"No, though I am finding out so much about him here lately."

Steven smiled and nodded. "I'm glad."

Julia was sitting there listening to Jake talk and thinking about Dan's newly awakened inner conflict about Joe. She also found it difficult to believe that Mike's spirit had come to her son and endowed him with special racing skills for a kid his age.

The light from the fire was getting dimmer, and Julia had a question. "Jake, do you feel any different since we've been here?"

"Yeah, I feel more in tune to Mike McConnell's spirit. It's really weird and hard to explain. At first, I thought I was going crazy or insane. I was thinking back when this all started. I was gradually gaining interest in Mike when he was on TV and having visions of him. Then all of a sudden, I discover this unforeseen talent, plus seeing ghosts and talking to them. It's finally all making sense to me what my purpose is and why this is all happening. I don't feel like I'm going insane anymore. And I now can accept the fact of what is happening."

Julia nodded. She replied, "Isn't it strange how another spirit can be within you. I've read about this happening, that people have remembered something about a past life, that they possibly had been at a certain place before as a different person. I've also read before about a little boy remembering that he was a World War II pilot. He actually remembered the pilot's name and where he crashed. But I never read that a person can take on the physical abilities that the other person used to have. It's obviously happening here, but it's all so strange to me. I too can accept the fact that what is happening here is real. And, Dan, I'm concerned about the inner conflict you're having about Joe and the way things were unresolved before he died."

Dan started speaking. "I agree with everything you've said. Yes, this newly awakened feeling about my father has stirred up inside me, but I can deal with it. I appreciate the concern. And, Jake, everything that brought us here obviously was no accident. I'm glad to hear that you've accepted what is happening and you don't think you're going insane. It's really getting late. I think we should all turn in for the night."

"Good night, Pearsons," said Steven.

"Good night, Steven," they replied.

***

Saturday morning, everyone started repairing the broken-down racetrack. The Pearsons got to painting the old place. There was so much activity going on, it started drawing the attention of the local people.

The sheriff noticed a little activity going on at the racetrack. He was seeing people coming and going out of there with paint and supplies, so he decided to drive over to the hardware store to see if anyone knew anything.

After checking with the store owner, he discovered some people were acting strange when buying a bunch of paint and supplies. Everyone in the store started to get excited that maybe the track would be reopening so they contacted the local news station to report a possible story.

***

Back at the racetrack, the cement company showed up on Monday morning, and they were moving along really fast. "I think we can have this done by tonight," said the concrete foreman.

"That would be great. How long do we have to wait before we can race on it?" asked Dan.

"Give it a good week to settle in and dry up."

"A week? We have to wait a week?" asked Dan.

"Go ahead and get on it. Then you will have us back to fix it!"

"No, we will wait a week," said Steven as he placed his hand on Dan's shoulder.

Dan nodded with a sulky look on his face.

That afternoon, an unexpected TV news crew showed up.

"Look who's here," Jake said with a big smile on his face.

The news reporter walked up to Jake. "Excuse me, little boy. Is Steven Webster around somewhere?"

"Little boy?" *Okay*, Jake said to himself. Then he put his finger by his chin and said, "Mmm, let me see. What does he look like?"

"I'm not sure," she said.

"Well, how would you know if I steered you wrong if you don't know what he looks like?"

"I don't know. I'm sorry if I offended you by calling you a little boy," she said.

"No problem. He is over there," he said, pointing at his dad.

"Okay, thank you," she said.

Dan was talking to Julia. They were over on the other side of the racetrack. Dan noticed a lady talking to Jake. He waved to her, and she walked over to them.

"Mr. Webster, I am Molly Smith from the local news Channel 3. I would like to do a story on the new development here at Wilkesboro Speedway."

"Well, I would love to give you a story, but I am not Mr. Webster," said Dan.

"Well, this is embarrassing. Do you know where he is? Can I speak to him?" she asked.

"He's taking a nap, and he is not to be disturbed," said Julia.

"Okay. May I come back another time?" she asked.

"Be my guest," said Dan.

"Thank you." She walked by Jake, giving him a mean look.

"Have a nice day," Jake said with a grin on his face.

Steven came out from the announcer's booth. "Is she gone?"

"How did you know she was here?" Vinci asked.

"I heard Jake say, 'Look who's here,' and I figured it was nobody I wanted to speak to."

"She'll be back," said Jake.

"I figured," said Steven with a disgusted look on his face.

***

Keith Herman whipped his semitrailer around in front of their storage garage at M-40 Speedway.

"We're gonna have to take two car carriers. Are you up to driving one, Dee, or should I ask someone else?" asked Keith.

"Yes, I can drive one. That's not a problem. I'm glad I kept my CDL license up to date."

Keith and Dee had a total of six late-model cars in their garage, and they were also able to borrow six from their friends.

"North Wilkesboro, Dee. That track used to pack the people," said Keith.

"Yeah, it's exciting, hon. I don't understand why the owner could not find any race cars closer. And why isn't NASCAR helping them out?" she commented.

"Maybe the owner lost contact with all the drivers because the track has been closed for so long. And maybe NASCAR will be the last to find out about it because he is upset at them. Who knows? All I know is we were asked to help them out, and I think we should."

Dee nodded. "I agree; it's just questions going through my mind," she said.

"I understand," replied Keith. "How about we go get a bite to eat, catch a nap, and then hit the road about 1:00 a.m. when there is no traffic?"

"Great idea," she replied.

By the end of a long day, the racetrack looked brighter and newer than it did when it was first built.

"I am amazed how much we got done today," Dan mumbled, noting the pain in his arms.

Vinci was lying in her mom's arms snoring.

"I need to get you to bed, little girl." Julia lifted Vinci up to her chest and started walking back to the house. "Good night, everybody," she said.

"Good night," replied Dan, Jake, and Steven.

The guys started walking around the racetrack, assessing what needed to be done tomorrow. Jake walked by the gate, placed his palm on the door, closed his eyes, and waited.

Dan and Steven stood back and observed him. He took his hand off the door and had an upset look on his face.

"What is it?" they asked.

"I thought I would feel something, but nothing came to me." He was very disappointed.

"You're just tired, and it's late. Why don't you go crash for the night?" replied Dan.

Jake had a funny look on his face. "Is that supposed to be funny, Dad?" he said with a half-crooked smile.

Steven burst out laughing. "This isn't the place to talk about crashing."

Dan had a silly look on his face. "Yeah, I guess you're right."

The guys walked slowly back to the house under a full moon's light. They took their time walking back to the house before turning in for the night.

***

The next day, Keith and Dee pulled into North Wilkesboro. They had no trouble finding their way down. The townspeople noticed the semitruck with a dozen race cars pulling into the racetrack. That raised their suspicions up even higher.

Dan greeted Keith and Dee with a huge hug of appreciation. He introduced them to Steven. He really showed his appreciation, also.

"You guys are just in time. I am cooking on the grill," said Dan.

"Great. We are starved," said Keith and Dee.

"After lunch, we can unload the cars," said Keith.

"Cool! Sounds good," said Jake.

Dan cooked up some T-bone and porterhouse steaks with a Caesar salad and corn on the cob.

"Looks like dinnertime instead of lunchtime," said Dee, while her stomach growled.

Julia started laughing. "Every time Dan cooks on the grill, he overdoes it with too much food."

Lunch was served, and everybody pulled up a bucket or some kind of seat by the racetrack. They all got in a circle like they were having a campfire and enjoyed their lunch.

"Steven, the racetrack looks good," said Keith. He was surprised they got it done so quickly.

"Thank you. The cement crew did an awesome job."

"The paint job is looking good, also," said Dee.

"Yeah, everybody has been working like little bees around here," said Dan.

"That concrete is going to be green for a few days," said Keith.

"They recommend we stay off the track for a week," said Jake.

"A week? Then what is the hurry for us to get the cars down here?" asked Keith with suspicion.

"We are expecting some guests," said Jake.

"Oh, yeah? What kind of guests?" he asked.

Jake looked around and saw everybody staring at him, waiting for his next answer.

"Some past heroes."

"Oh, yeah, like Richard Petty?"

"No, older than that."

Keith had a funny look on his face. "What are you talking about, Jake?"

"It's going to be a huge celebration, and you're welcome to stay if you would like, but we need to wait a week for the track," said Steven.

"We still have plenty of painting to do," said Dan, grabbing a paintbrush that was lying beside him and lifting it in the air.

"You guys are not going to tell us, are you?" Keith asked.

"They're going to make us wait?" Dee exclaimed, mixed emotions charging through her head.

"There is an extra house on the property. You can stay there if you want," replied Steven.

Keith and Dee spoke very quietly between themselves, discussing who would be taking care of business back home, running their racetrack and managing their affairs. They were also suspicious of the secrecy. They had a good feeling that something cool was going to happen. "Okay, we will stay and see the big celebration and whatever the hoopla is," said Keith.

"Great." Dan stood up from his can and threw his hands in the air. "We can start painting after lunch."

8

The Time Is Now

Hank Walters, the president of NASCAR, was sitting at his desk doing paperwork when his secretary came in and said she'd just gotten a weird phone call about the track in Wilkesboro.

"I guess there's some activity going on that we need to see."

Hank's associates were wondering what it could be. "Well, let's go down there."

"Let's wait a few days, and then we will check it out," said Hank.

***

Steven was standing in the middle of Wilkesboro, looking around and thinking about how fast that one week had gone by. He was so proud of howeverybody worked very hard to get the racetrack looking good. It had a fresh coat of paint put on all the buildings. All the restrooms were in good working order, and all the bleachers were extra secured. The place looked brand new again.

"I am so proud of everybody—Jake, Dan, Julia, Vinci, Keith, and Dee. I am just amazed at what you've accomplished in just one week. I think we are ready to get the race cars on the track for our company," said Steven.

"That's a great idea. Let's put them on pit row," Jake replied enthusiastically.

"Good idea," said Steven, giving Jake a thumbs-up.

Keith, Dee, and Dan brought the cars from the back, drove them onto the track, and lined them up on pit row like Jake said.

"It's perfect!" Jake replied.

After all the cars were brought on pit row, Steven said to Jake, "Well, I think we're ready."

"Ready for what?" he asked.

"The big bamboozo. The opening of the gate."

Jake wasn't sure what to say. He started to feel a little nervous. His palms were getting sweaty. His forehead was becoming hot, and he was feeling a little faint.

"Jake, honey, you don't look good." Julia grabbed his right arm and helped him sit down. His legs were shaking uncontrollably.

"Jake, are you okay?" Dan asked, very concerned. He placed his hand on Jake's legs.

"I am just a little overwhelmed right now," Jake replied, rubbing his forehead and getting some of the sweat off.

"Why don't we go back to the house for a while? We can come back later," said Julia.

He took a deep breath and then exhaled the air from his lungs. "No, I want to do this. I don't want to wait," he said to everybody.

Jake stood up very slowly. His dad had a hold of his hand and his arm, helping him up.

He regained his composure. "Okay, I'm ready. Let's go over to the gate."

Everybody walked over to the gate and stared at it for a while. To Jake, the gate looked one hundred feet tall. For a little boy, waiting with expectation and wonder, to take control of other spirits' destinies was one big burden. To others, it was a glorious wonder.

"Well, this is what we've been waiting for," said Dee.

They all waited with the biggest anticipation. "Well, Jake, open it up," Steven said.

Jake grabbed the gate with both hands. His palms were very sweaty. He leaned back and started pulling the gate open. He struggled a little bit. Keith offered to help, but he was told he could not help. Keith did not understand what was happening at the time and why he couldn't help. Jake slowly pulled the gate open. Once he got it totally open, everybody stood and stared at the woods.

"What is supposed to happen next?" Dee asked.

Everybody was quiet and kept staring at the woods for a good five minutes.

"I don't get it. Where are they?" Steven said.

"Yeah, where is everybody?" Vinci asked.

Dan and Julia had puzzled looks on their faces.

"What are we watching for?" Keith asked.

"They are supposed to come from over there," Jake said as he pointed at the woods and then up through the field to the racetrack. "This is the only way in."

"Who is?" Dee asked, very suspiciously.

"The past NASCAR greats," Jake said.

Keith started laughing. "Are you kidding me? We did all this for some ghost? Are you guys crazy?"

"No, we are not," Jake said with an angry look on his face.

"Let's go back to the house and explain to Keith and Dee what we are waiting for," said Steven.

"Good idea. I wish somebody would explain what's going on," Keith said.

Everybody went back except for Jake. Jake stayed at the gate and continued to stare at the woods as if he were on guard duty.

Evening time came. Julia went outside to see if she could talk Jake into coming inside for the night.

"Come on, Jake. We will leave the gate open. They will show up when they are ready."

Jake looked really frustrated and confused. "Okay, Mom. Why didn't they come when the gate opened up?" he asked with disappointment.

"I'm not sure, honey, but I believe they will when they're ready."

Jake nodded, agreeing with his mom. He grasped his mom's hand and walked back to the house to get ready for bed.

Keith and Dee were truly amazed by the story about Jake's past life.

"I think we're going to stick around and see what happens. Besides, you have our cars," Keith said.

"That's no problem. I have a feeling that things are going to get good," Dan commented.

Three days went by, and no spirit had walked out of the woods. The Pearsons were starting to get concerned about

Jake missing all the races that were scheduled. They were starting to get frustrated with each other, feeling that no spirit was actually ever going to walk out of the woods and onto the racetrack. They were questioning if they had made a wrong decision.

The NASCAR president, Hank Walters, visited North Wilkesboro Speedway. He was so impressed by the improvements that he made an offer to Steven to buy the racetrack. Steven seriously considered it. Dan got very angry with Steven because he was even considering it. Dan knew if he sold it, then all the work they did was for nothing.

The Pearsons were packed up and ready to leave for home that night.

"Hey, Dad, you know what I would like to do is race that brand-new kart around the track before we leave."

"You bet, buddy. I'm sorry that we haven't had it out with everything else going on."

"It's okay. We have been busy; plus I've had the smaller kart out a few times. I understand," said Jake.***

Dan and Jake went inside the trailer and got out the brand-new Rotax kart with a thirty-nine horsepower engine that would reach a top speed of sixty-five to seventy miles per hour.

"Now, Jake, this kart is much faster. Start out slow to get a good feel of it before opening it up top speed."

"Okay, Dad," Jake replied.

Jake started out slowly at thirty-five miles per hour, listening to his dad's advice.

Jake drove by his dad with his right thumb up, and his dad gave him a thumbs-up in return.

Steven walked up, stood by Dan, and watched Jake warm up around the track.

"He's going to like the speed in that kart!" replied Steven.

"Yes, he will. I told him to start out slow and slowly build up the speed. I'm glad he's following my advice."

"Dan, if I sell the track, you will get paid back everything you have invested into it," said Steven.

"I know, Steven. It's just frustrating because it all seemed right to do this, and you were so sure about them coming."

Julia, Vinci, Keith, and Dee walked out to the trackside to watch Jake race around the track.

***

Jake had an audience, and he thought, *It's time to see how fast this kart can go.* Jake heard Mike's McConnell voice saying, "You need to be careful. The turns sneak up on you."

Jake pushed the kart to go faster and faster, until it was at the limits of its speed range. Jake knew he was going too fast, but for some reason, he didn't care. He gripped the wheel so hard his hands hurt. Sweat poured down his face and was immediately whipped away. His heart raced. The engine roared. The turns came on fast.

"Slow down, boy!" Jake heard Mike's voice in his head, loud and clear. "Slow down, Jake! Slow down right now before you get yourself killed!" Jake slowed way down because of Mike's warning but still lost control of the kart at just the wrong moment. He drove the front of his kart right into turn 2, crushing the whole front end. The wreck happened in the exact same place where Mike McConnell crashed.

"*Jake*?" Julia screamed as she started running to the wrecked kart.

Jake was lying still in the kart. He was not sure if he should move, just in case something was broken.

Then, all of a sudden, he felt Mike McConnell's spirit leave his body. Jake felt a sudden sickness come over him and vomited all over the steering wheel. Everybody else ran over to Jake's rescue. Dan unhooked his seat belt and removed his helmet.

"Jake, are you okay?"

Jake had vomit dripping off his chin. He wiped it off with his sleeve, nodded, and said, "Yeah, I'm fine."

"Does anything feel broken?" asked Steven.

"No, I'm fine. Something did happen when I wrecked."

"Yeah, what is it?" asked Julia.

"Mike McConnell is not with me anymore. I felt his spirit leave me!"

"Really? You felt that?" asked Steven.

"Yeah, he is not with me. I am sure of it."

Julia rubbed his head, relieved that he was okay. Jake got out of the kart and stood up, facing the gate. He noticed a shadow of a man standing there.

He pointed. "Look over there. Somebody is over there!"

They all turned their heads toward the gate and saw the same thing Jake saw.

"Excuse me, can we help you?" asked Steven.

The man walked out of the shadows and into the light where people could see him. When he got into a lighted area, Dan and Julia gasped.

"Oh my gosh, Dan. It's your father," Julia said.

Dan covered his mouth with his right hand. His eyes were wide open, and suddenly tears were rolling down his face.

There stood Dan's father. He looked the exact same way as in the picture at Steven's house—young and full of energy.

"Look at him, Julia. He does not look tired and worn down."

Julia grabbed Dan's arm with excitement. "Go talk to him," she said quietly.

***

Joe Pearson was a little unsure of where he was. He was looking around, amazed that he was standing at North Wilkesboro Speedway and that his son was also there.

Dan had so much emotion going through him, and yet to get to see his father again was a dream come true.

"Dad?" Dan said in a timid voice.

Joe Pearson walked up to his son. He placed his right hand on his cheek. "Son, it's been a long time. I've missed you!"

"Is this really you?"

"It is I."

They wrapped their arms around each other and embraced for a long time.

"I can't believe I can touch you," replied Dan.

"It's the magic of this racetrack. Dreams come true here," Steve commented.

Joe looked at his grandson, concerned about him. "Jake, are you okay from your wreck?"

"Yeah, I'm fine, Grandpa." Jake reached out and hugged him. "I'm amazed, as everybody else is, that you're actually here."

"I hear you've been breaking my racing records."

Everybody laughed.

"About time somebody beat them," he replied.

"I had a little help." Jake smirked.

"I think we need to go inside and let Dan and his father do some catching up," said Julia.

Everybody agreed. As they walked by Joe, Vinci grabbed his hand and said, "Hi, Grandpa."

"Hi, sweet Vinci." He then placed his hand on top of her head, and she smiled at him.

"You are one beautiful little girl."

"Thank you, Grandpa."

Keith grabbed Julia's arm when they were walking back to the house. "I can't believe what is happening," he whispered quietly and enthusiastically.

"I know! This is really happening. It's true," said Julia.

"He looked just as I remembered him," replied Steven.

Dee grabbed Keith's hand really tightly as they walked back together.

***

"I don't remember this place looking so nice," said Joe.

"Yes, we fixed it up for you," replied Dan.

"You guys did a nice job."

"Thank you, Dad."

"I was told you guys were waiting for me. I could not find my way here until I heard a race car in the distance. I followed the noise, and it led me here," said Joe.

"That's why it took so long. Because you were lost?"

"Yes, I came from far away to be here," he continued. "I am so glad you listened to Jake and followed him on his journey."

"I am too. I never knew how much you actually loved racing," commented Dan.

Joe was looking at the late-model cars. "Can I take one out for a ride?"

Dan smiled really big and tried to keep from crying. "Sure can. That's why they're here, for you," he replied. "Dad?" he said quietly.

"Yeah, son?"

"I'm sorry."

"Why are you sorry, son?"

"Holding you back from your dream."

"Dan, you never did that. You were the best thing that ever came into my life. You never held me back. My fear is what held me back." Joe placed his hands on his shoulders. "I love you, son."

Dan had tears rolling down his face. "I love you too, Dad."

Joe removed his hands from Dan's shoulders, walked over to the late-model race car, and gave it a good look-over. "They have changed a little since I've raced."

Dan smiled. "Get in and take her for a spin."

"I think we need to get Jake's kart off the track first," said Joe.

"Oh, yeah. That would be a good idea. I'll get it. You go ahead and get in the car."

Joe lifted his right leg up through the window and jumped inside the car. Once inside the car, he put on the helmet that was sitting off to the side. He secured himself into the seat and started the engine. He then drove the car onto the racetrack. Dan's family and friends could see Joe racing on the racetrack, so they came out of the house to watch him. Everybody took a seat in the Junior Johnson bleacher section. Dan walked out of pit row and joined his family.

***

"Wow, he is good!" Dan said with excitement.

"Yes, he really is," Steven said, remembering back in the day when he raced.

"Go, Grandpa!" Jake said, pumping his fist.

"I can't believe this is really happening. My dad is out there running a late-model race car, and we are watching him. Who would've thought this could be possible?"

Julia smiled at Dan. She snuggled really close to him, grabbed his left arm, and placed it around her shoulders.

"It's magical," Julia said.

They could see Joe flying around the track with ease, looking like a professional.

Joe raced the car around the racetrack fifty times. He enjoyed every minute in the car. He brought the car down to pit row and parked it. He took the helmet off and placed it off to the side. He then got out of the car and walked up to his family.

"Well, I should be going."

"What? Where are you going?" Dan asked.

"Back there." He pointed to the fence.

"Why? You can stay here."

Joe looked down at the track and shook his head.

"You can't leave outside the track, can you?" asked Steven.

"No, I can't." Joe then smiled. "I will be back tomorrow," he continued. "I have friends who would love to come here."

"Bring them. We did this for you guys," said Dan.

Joe nodded, and then he walked to the open gate. He looked back and waved to his family.

"Dad," Dan said with a crackling voice.

Joe looked back at Dan. "Yes, son?"

"I love you."

Joe smiled. "Love you, too. See you tomorrow."

Joe started walking through the field. When he got to the woods, he turned and waved. He took one step into the woods and started to vanish as he kept walking. Then suddenly, he was gone.

"Wow, that was cool!" Dee said.

"Honey, we're not going anywhere," Dan said to Julia.

Everybody started laughing.

"You think so? I thought you wanted to leave," Julia said with a big smile on her face.

Dan could see that Julia was picking on him. He grabbed her arm, picked her up, and spun her around.

"Put me down!" she screamed.

Dan put Julia down and walked over to Jake. He was really concerned about his wreck.

"How you doing, buddy? Do you feel okay?"

"Yeah, I'm fine. Just a little sore. I will be okay. That was really weird where I wrecked. The exact same place Mike McConnell wrecked."

"Yeah, I know. Are you sure Mike McConnell is not with you anymore?" Dan asked.

"Yeah, Dad, I'm sure. It was really weird when he left my body. I can tell a difference now."

"Do you think you can still race?" Julia asked.

"I don't have the desire to. It's different now."

"It's okay, buddy. We understand. You'll know if you want to," Dan commented.

Julia nodded, agreeing with Dan.

9

There Are Others

In Three Oaks, Michigan, Tony was sitting at his desk talking to Dan on the phone.

"It's been three weeks since we talked. What is the problem? Why haven't you been attending the races? And why haven't you been answering my calls?"

"It's really complicated," Dan replied.

"Try me, buddy," said Tony, frustrated at Dan.

"Why don't you get in your car and drive down to North Wilkesboro Speedway and see for yourself? It's better if you see for yourself. Then you will understand."

"I guess I will see you in a few hours." Tony was very upset. He packed up, loaded his vehicle, and headed south.

The next morning, Dan's father came back, and he brought some friends. They walked out of the woods and up through the field to the gate. Each driver cautiously walked onto the property. All twelve of them knew exactly where they were. Each of them had raced at North Wilkesboro Speedway at one time or another.

Joe pointed. "Over there, on pit row, are the cars. I will find the light switch to this place so we can get racing."

"I believe the light switch is on a pole down by pit row," said Red Byron.

Red walked down with Joe. They found the breaker switch. Red pulled down on the handle. The lights came on, and the whole place was lit up like it was daylight. The twelve NASCAR greats looked around at the racetrack.

"It's exactly how I remember it but newer looking," said Herb Thomas.

"Yeah, they really fixed the place up," said Joe Pearson.

"Take a look at these cars. They have changed," said Fireball Roberts.

"No, they're exactly how I remembered them. They're called late models," said Neil Bonnett.

"Maybe you remember them that way, but when I was racing, they did not look like this," replied Fireball.

"Well, you're a little older than me," commented Neil.

"Really? You think so?" said Fireball sarcastically.

Each driver picked the car he wanted to drive. They all got inside their cars and put on their helmets. Then they all started the engines. A huge rumbling noise went through the racetrack and outside the racetrack property.

Steven was startled from his sleep by the rumbling noise. He looked out his window, and he could see the lights were on at the racetrack. He walked into Julia and Dan's room.

"What is going on at the track?"

"I think they're back," Dan replied.

"It's four o'clock in the morning," Julia said.

"Well, they must have found the switch to the lights because those are on," said Steven.

Dan grabbed his shoes, and Julia grabbed her slippers and overcoat. Jake and Vinci grabbed their tennis shoes.

Keith and Dee were also awake from the rumbling. They slipped on some shoes. They all walked over to the racetrack, sat down in the Junior Johnson section, and watched them race around the track. The drivers were hooting and hollering. They were doing burnouts and doughnuts and driving like maniacs.

"I can't believe we are behind the wheel again," said Fireball Roberts.

"Woohoo! This is great!" said Neil Bonnett.

"I didn't think I would ever be able to do this again," said Joe Weatherly.

The cars were running around the track, occasionally bumping one another for fun.

After bumping and banging for an hour, the NASCAR greats wanted to take a rest. They drove down pit row, parked their cars, and got out of them.

They walked up to where everybody was sitting in Junior Johnson's section. They were wearing the old-style racing suits. The material was very thin and unlike the fire suits worn today. Each driver walked with confidence. Some were carrying their helmets alongside of them.

"Hi, Dad. I see you brought some friends," said Dan.

"Sorry about coming here so early. They just could not wait," said Joe.

"Thank you for everything you have done," said Fireball Roberts.

"You're welcome," replied Dan.

"Steven, do you mind if we have a little fifty-lap race?" asked Fireball.

"Heavens no. You can race as long as you want to. This place is reopened for you guys. No outsiders will be using this track any longer. This track is yours. Use it as much as you want," said Steven.

"Really? You're not kidding? We can use it anytime?" asked Bobby Isaac.

"Yes. Anytime," answered Steven with a big smile.

The NASCAR heroes all smiled and applauded them.

"Thank you very much," they said, with great appreciation. Then they all walked back with excitement to their cars to get ready for the race.

"You're going down, Fireball!" said Glen Wood.

Fireball smiled at him. "We'll see who goes down!"

All the cars were started at once. A huge roar went through the stands. Vinci and Julia covered their ears. Jake smiled really big.

"I love that sound," he said.

The cars pulled onto the track. They lined up two by two in a gentlemanly fashion since there was no qualifying.

They made three practice laps around the track before the race started.

"Vinci, would you like to wave the green flag for them?" asked Steven.

"You bet I would," she replied.

She took the flag from Steven, walked up to where the start/finish line was, and climbed up the little tower. All the drivers could see her. They all put their hands out the windows and waved as they drove by. Vinci waved back at them.

The cars came around on their last practice lap. They started to increase their speed when they were getting closer to the start/finish line. Vinci raised the green flag. She started to wave it back and forth. The drivers put their pedals to the metal and got on with the race.

Vinci brought the flag back to Steven. "Thank you very much. That was a blast." She had the biggest grin.

"You're welcome," he said with a smile.

"All those drivers are the top fifty best NASCAR drivers," said Steven.

"Is that right?" Keith asked.

"Yep." He continued on, "The first car has Neil Bonnett driving it. He won eighteen Winston Cup races. Butch Nelson, his longtime friend, said, 'When Bonnett got into a car, the car knew it was going to race.' He had a fatal crash on February 11, 1994, at the Daytona 500 practice.

"The second car has Red Byron in it. He holds a record that can never be broken. He was the first NASCAR points champion. Poor health forced him out of racing. He died of a heart attack at the age of forty-four.

"Then there is Bobby Isaac. He rose from poverty to become a NASCAR champion. He didn't own a pair of shoes until he was thirteen. He suffered a heart attack after getting out of his car during a two-hundred-lapper. He died early the next morning.

"Leeroy Yarbrough. If you were ahead of him, you'd better watch out. If you blinked too many times, he would pass you. One of the best things about him was he was not a dirty driver.

"Glen Wood. He founded the legendary Wood Brothers racing team in 1953. Herb Thomas. He raced 228 races over ten years: 48 wins, 156 top ten, and 39 poles. Marshall Teague also died on February 11 in 1959 at the Daytona International Speedway. He died while attempting a closed-course speed record in a reconfigured Indy car, eleven days before the first Daytona 500. The test session was in preparation for the April debut of the United States Auto Club Championship with the Indy-style roadsters. His car spun and flipped through the third turn, and Teague was thrown, seat and all, from his car. He died almost instantly. And Fireball Roberts—" Steven was interrupted.

"Jake told us about him at lunch one day," Tony replied from behind the stands. He then peeked around the corner so they could see him.

Everybody turned and yelled, "Tony?"

"Hey, guys, what's happening?"

"You got down here quick," Dan said.

"Yeah, I drove with the pedal to the metal. I had to see what the big deal was and why all the secrecy." He then continued on, "I see you're watching a race."

"Yeah, come and have a seat," said Dan. He then slid down from where he was sitting to make room for Tony.

"These guys are pretty good. Where did they come from?"

"They came from far away," replied Jake.

"This place looks brand new. Did you guys do this?"

"Yeah, we worked very hard on the place," commented Dan.

"And it sure was worth it," replied Julia.

Each driver led in front for at least a half of a lap. It was a very calm race until the last two laps, and then it was a free-for-all—each man for himself.

There was a lot of bumping and banging done in the last two laps. Some tempers even flew. The end result winner was Joe Pearson. He dodged and weaved through traffic and avoided getting into any conflicts. He pulled the biggest burnout ever in his victory lap. The rest of the drivers pulled down to pit row and got out of their cars.

Tony had a shocked look on his face. His back arched up from where he was sitting. He pointed at pit row. "Look who is out there! That's Marshall Teague and Curtis Turner, Joe Weatherly, Tiny Lund. And there is your dad, Joe Pearson! Dan, what is going on here?" he continued. "Why are they dressed up like old NASCAR greats? Can you tell me what's going on?"

"Yeah, Tony, I will tell you." He started explaining everything to him.

While Dan was explaining to Tony, the NASCAR greats were back on the racetrack, taking some warm-up laps before their next race.

"We decided to do some more racing!" yelled Fireball from his car to Steven and Dan and the rest of the gang.

Steven gave a thumbs-up and yelled back at Fireball, "I will control the lap counter."

Fireball put his hand out the window while driving around the track and gave Steven a thumbs-up in return.

"Keith and Dee, can you start the race?" asked Steven.

"Heck, yeah. I'd love to watch those guys race again," replied Keith.

Dee had the green flag in her hand. She raised the flag and started waving it back and forth. The race cars came around turn 4, and the drivers saw Dee waving the flag. They put the pedal to the metal and got the race started. Everybody was so excited, watching the race unfold. They just could not believe that it was really happening.

"This place is magical," Julia said to Vinci.

"I know, Mom. Isn't it cool watching Grandpa out there?"

Tony started talking to Dan. "Now I understand why Jake had so much talent. Who even knew that Mike McConnell's spirit was with him? There were times I would question why this kid was so good and how he knew so much about racing? It all makes sense now."

"Tony, you were meant to be here. Joe Pearson raced at your track, and he still holds records there. I could have gone to any go-kart dealer that day, but I was led to you," said Dan.

Tony nodded. "You know, I followed a lot of these guys while they were racing in the Cup Series. These guys are heroes to thousands of people. Their fans would love to see them again," he said.

"Heavens, yes. We're going to let the public see them race," said Dan.

"Really? That's great! They need to see this place. It's magical. People will feel good when they leave here. It will give them an inner peace. And people who are not race fans will come and watch and be amazed. They will feel the magic this place has. It will be good for everybody," commented Tony.

"I can't agree more," replied Dan.

"Let me handle the president of Birel. We'll get you out of that contract," said Tony.

"Thank you, Tony. That would be great," said Dan.

The fifty-lap race was coming to a finish, and Joe Pearson took the checkered flag again.

"Way to go, Dad!" Dan and his family were cheering for him.

"You the man, Grandpa," said Vinci.

"Way to take the checkered flag again," said Jake.

The NASCAR greats pulled their cars down to pit row and parked them. They were all excited to be racing again.

"Let's go down there and visit with them," said Jake.

"Really? We can go down there?" asked Tony.

Dan stood up from his seat. "Heck, yeah. Let's go."

Everybody walked down to pit row and visited with the drivers. Tony acted like a little giggly schoolgirl who had just seen her first love. "Man, I need to get ahold of myself," said Tony.

"You're okay. I think I would act the same way if I just saw a bunch of ghosts racing," replied Curtis Turner, one of the NASCAR greats.

"We let the rookie win," said Neil Bonnett.

Everybody laughed.

"That was the coolest race I have ever seen," said Tony.

"Yeah, we have a little bit of experience," said Tiny Lund with a little grin on his face.

Everybody cracked up laughing.

"We're going to leave, but we will be back later today," said Dan's father.

"Okay, you guys, we will see you later," said Steven.

The NASCAR greats started to leave. Dan had enjoyed watching his father race. He started feeling a lot of emotions going through him, watching his father walk away.

"Hey, Dad," he said with a cracking voice.

Joe Pearson turned around and looked at his son. "Yeah, son?"

"I love you." His voice was very faint.

Joe walked back to his son and looked him in the eye. He could see tears rolling down his face. He opened his arms up, and they embraced each other. "I have missed you so much, son, and I am so very proud of you. I love you."

They took a moment, enjoying being in each other's arms.

"I will be back soon," he whispered.

Dan nodded. He let go of his father and watched him walk away. The NASCAR greats waited for Joe by the gate with respect.

"We will see you soon!" yelled Red to the others.

They all left through the gate, walked through the field, and faded into the woods.

"Wow! What a morning this has been!" said Dee.

"Yes, what a morning!" replied Dan.

Everybody agreed.

"I am going to put on some breakfast," said Julia.

"Okay, I will help," replied Dee.

"Would anybody want to help me fuel these cars back up?" asked Steven.

"Yeah, sure," Keith, Dan, and Tony answered with enthusiasm.

10

Time to Go Home

Dan and Steve stayed at the track fueling up the cars and getting ready for the next race.

"I wonder what they do when they leave, and where do they go?" said Dan.

"Good question. I wonder also," Steve replied. "Everything looks good, and we're ready for them next time."

The president from NASCAR, Hank Walters, showed up to see if Steven was ready to sell the racetrack. Also, the news reporter returned at the same time.

"Howdy, ma'am," said Hank.

"Howdy, sir," she said.

He walked into the racetrack area and found Steven, and she followed him.

"Who is your friend?" Steven asked Hank.

"I don't know her. She did not come with me," he said.

"Hi, I'm Steven." He extended his hand to her.

"Hi, I'm Molly Smith from local news Channel 3," she said, shaking his hand.

"Give me a moment, Molly. I need to speak to this gentleman."

"Hank, I'm not interested anymore in selling the racetrack," he said.

"What? I don't understand. What changed your mind?"

"They did." He pointed at the NASCAR greats, as they were walking back to their cars.

"Why, that's Tiny Lund, Joe Weatherly, Curtis Turner, Neil Bonnett, Red Byron, Bobby Isaac, Leeroy Yarbrough, Glen Wood, Herb Thomas, Fireball Roberts, Marshall Teague … but I don't know that one guy."

"His name is Joe Pearson."

"Is this some type of joke?"

"No, it's no joke. They have come back to race here. That's why we fixed this place up for them. I was not sure if they were going to come; that's why I was considering your offer. But then they showed up. This place is not for sale any longer."

"Can I stay and watch them?"

"You sure can."

"May I stay, too?" asked Molly Smith.

"You can even do a story if you want to."

"Really? Great. Thank you," she said very excitedly.

The NASCAR greats were back on the racetrack, racing, bumping, and banging. The rest of the gang sat down in the Junior Johnson section, very excited that they were back.

Steven invited Hank and Molly to join them where everybody else was sitting.

They walked over and joined the rest of the gang. Molly remembered Jake from before. She wrinkled her nose at him, and he waved back at her with a huge smile.

"Joe Pearson won the race this morning," said Jim to Hank Walters.

"This is amazing. They're ghost racing real cars."

"They can touch you, and you can touch them. They don't feel like ghosts," said Steven.

"You think they would remember me?" asked Hank Walters.

"Oh, yeah," replied Dan.

"When they are back in pit row, we'll go down there," said Dan.

"Okay, I can't wait," said Hank very excitedly.

After forty-five minutes of racing, all the racers pulled into pit row for a little break. Steven, Hank, Molly, Dan, Julia, Jake, Vinci, Dee, and Keith walked down to visit with them.

"Hey, guys," said Hank.

"Well, look who's here!" said Neil Bonnett.

"Hey, Hank, it's been a long time," said Leeroy Yarbrough.

Leeroy extended his hand to shake Hank's. Hank put his hand out slowly.

"Don't worry; you won't catch anything," said Leeroy with a big smile.

"I'm sorry." Then Hank put his hand out to shake. "I just can't believe this. All you guys are here," said Hank.

"Oh, there are more coming. The word is getting out," said Fireball.

"Hank, you're not retired yet?" asked Marshall Teague.

Hank laughed. "No, not yet."

"Would you guys like to drive some Sprint Cup cars?" asked Hank.

"Heck yeah!" said Neil.

"What are those?" asked Herb Thomas.

"They are the newer-style stock car. You'll love them!" replied Neil.

"Okay, we'll have them here in a few days, ready to race."

"All right," everybody cheered.

Molly was reporting everything. "This is going to make the five o'clock news. People are going to be amazed!" she said.

Steven nodded. "Yes, they will."

"Well, I need to get some cars here, so I'm going to leave for now. You guys enjoy your day, and I will see you soon," said Hank.

"Okay, Hank. Thank you," said all the NASCAR greats.

***

Molly was on TV at five o'clock. She was reporting about the North Wilkesboro Speedway. She reported everything about the NASCAR greats and how it all happened because of a little boy by the name of Jake Pearson and a famous NASCAR driver by the name of Mike McConnell. The story traveled around quickly to all the big television stations. All the major news stations were traveling to North Wilkesboro Speedway to report about the past NASCAR greats.

That evening, a line of cars' headlights lined up for many miles, traveling to the racetrack.

"You see? They're all coming," replied Steven.

"Yeah, they are," answered Dan with a glowing smile.

"Well, Julia, I think it's time to go back home," said Dan.

"What about your dad?" asked Julia.

"It's time to go. We need to get back home and take care of what we left there. We'll be back soon," he said.

Julia thought about what Dan had said. "Yeah, you're right. It's time."

The Pearsons got packed up and were saying goodbye to everybody.

"Will you be back soon?" asked Steven.

"You bet. I have to see my dad," Dan said with a smile.

"I think somebody wants to say goodbye." Steven pointed at Dan's father standing by the gate.

Dan walked over to the gate slowly, enjoying every minute he had spent with his father. He got choked up trying to talk. Tears were starting to roll down his cheeks.

"Hi, Dad."

"Hi, son."

"It's time we go back home."

"I know, son."

"I have enjoyed the time together, Dad."

"So have I, son."

They hugged each other for a long time.

"We'll be back very soon. And we're going to visit very often."

"Sounds good, son."

Julia, Jake, and Vinci said their goodbyes. Joe hugged each one of them. When he got to Jake, he hugged him for a long time.

"Jake, somebody wants to say goodbye to you," said Joe.

"Okay, who is it?"

Out from behind the gate walked a NASCAR great; he stood there with a smile.

"Jake, do you know who I am?"

"Yes, you're Mike McConnell."

He nodded. "Jake, thank you for listening to my spirit and taking the journey we did together. I will always be grateful to you, and so will all the other NASCAR greats."

"You're welcome, Mike. I would do it again if needed." They hugged and said goodbye to each other.

"Well, Keith, Dee, and Tony, are you guys ready to start making some money? We're going to have some company real soon," said Steven.

The Pearsons pulled away from the racetrack, and a line of cars was pulling in. The line went on for miles and miles. They came from far away.

"Dad, wait! Can we go back? I would like to watch Mike McConnell race one time before we leave," asked Jake.

"Yes, I think we can do that for one race," said Dan.

***

The stands were completely full of fans. All the fans were talking among themselves and to others.

"You can feel the magic in the air," said someone.

"Look! There's Mike McConnell and all the NASCAR greats," someone else said.

The cars pulled out of pit row and onto the track. They did a two-lap warm-up, and then the race started. The race took the fans back to the days they remembered.

Everything had changed with the supernatural things that were happening. They were unexplainable, but no one cared because they were enjoying something magical.

The cars flew around the track at a top speed. There were flashes of light from the cars. Each of the drivers had a little fun bumping and banning, sharing a little paint with one another. Mike McConnell led the race. He remembered the fatal wall as he flew by it. He mumbled to himself, "Let's not do that again."

Jake felt a special connection to Mike, watching him. "I'm glad we came back to see this," said Jake.

"Yeah! We are too," said Dan.

Julia and Vinci nodded, agreeing with Dan.

The magical race came to an end with Mike McConnell winning. He pulled his car right in front of where Jake was sitting. Mike got out of the car and took a bow right at Jake. He then touched his heart with his right fist and lightly pounded on it. Then he pointed at Jake. "Thank you, Jake!" he yelled up at him.

Jake did the same back to Mike McConnell. "You're welcome!"

***

The fans filled the stands every day. And when they left, they had a good feeling about themselves. They felt whatever was wrong in the world, this place made it right!

Afterword

The picture shown at the beginning of each chapter was taken during the end stage of the book at Warren Dunes State Park in Michigan. What amazed me about the picture was the Spirit Orb that showed up in the photo. Also, Warren Dunes State Park is mentioned in the book so I felt it was appropriate to insert the photo.

The book came into being with my father in mind. His favorite movie was the Field of Dreams. Every time he watched it He cried. So I was inspired to write something similar to that.

I always wanted me and my son to get into racing yet I Couldn't come up with enough money to get started in it. So we became fans of the sport instead. In the early stages when Jake, started racing I was written about something I wish I could have done with my son. So it was a real joy bringing that to being.

When written the book I had my family in mind. My wife is a third grade teacher and my two children my son being the oldest of my daughter which I'm very proud of all of them.

WM TODD NICHOLS

Printed and bound by PG in the USA